P9-BJW-020

CHABOT COLLEGE-HAYWARD

2 555 000 017705 .

68062   PR
                         1184
Cole   C72

A book of love poems

DATE DUE		
FEB 8 '99		
OCT 0 2 2002		
APR 1 4 2004		
SEP 3 0 2008		
9/15/10		

COLLEGE
MAY 1 8 '95
LIBRARY

OCT 21 '82

NOV 11 '82

FEB 22 '83

MAR 18 '83

MAR 1 6 '95

PRINTED IN U.S.A.

25555 Hesperian Boulevard
Hayward, California 94545

A Book of Love Poems

A Book of Love Poems

Edited by WILLIAM COLE

Illustrated by Lars Bo

The Viking Press   New York

ΓR
1184
C72

Copyright © 1965 by William Cole
All rights reserved
First published in 1965 by The Viking Press, Inc.
625 Madison Avenue, New York, N. Y. 10022
Published simultaneously in Canada by
The Macmillan Company of Canada Limited

SECOND PRINTING JULY *1966*

Library of Congress catalog card number: 65-18158

808.81   1. Poetry—Collections
           2. Love poetry

PRINTED IN THE U. S. A. BY MONTAUK BOOK MFG. CO., INC.

Acknowledgments

Acknowledgment is made to the following publishers and authors or their representatives for their permission to use copyright material. Every reasonable effort has been made to clear the use of the poems in this volume with the copyright owners. If notified of any omissions the editor and publisher will gladly make the proper corrections in future editions.

Ernest Benn Limited, for "Were You on the Mountain?" translated by Douglas Hyde from *Love Songs of Connaght.*
Beth Bentley, for her poem "A Waltz in the Afternoon."
Mrs. Jethro Bithell, for "Spring" (translated by Jethro Bithell) by Andre Spire.
Robert Bly, for his poem "Love Poem" from *Silence in the Snowy Fields* (Wesleyan University Press, 1962; copyright 1962 by Robert Bly).
The Bodley Head Ltd., for "Donall Oge" by Lady Augusta Gregory and "Lily McQueen" by Sara Jackson from *The Distaff Muse.*
Margaret Conklin, Literary Executor, Estate of Sara Teasdale, for "Young Love" from *Helen of Troy.*
The Cresset Press Limited, for "The Corner of the Field" from *Collected Poems* by Frances Cornford; and for "Winter" from *A Kite's Dinner* by Sheila Wingfield.
Edwin Denby for his poem "A Girl" from *In Public in Private.*
Dodd, Mead and Company and McClelland and Stewart Limited, for "The

Hill" and "There's Wisdom in Women" from *The Collected Poems of Rupert Brooke* (copyright 1915 by Dodd, Mead and Company; copyright 1943 by Edward Marsh).

Doubleday and Company, Inc., for "When One Loves Tensely" from *Love Sonnets of a Cave Man* by Don Marquis (copyright 1921 by Sun Printing and Publishing Assoc.); and for "She" from *Words for the Wind* by Theodore Roethke (copyright © 1956 by Theodore Roethke).

Gerald Duckworth and Company Limited, for "Sea Love" from *Collected Poems* by Charlotte Mew.

E. P. Dutton and Company, Inc. for "Mexican Serenade" from *Lyric Laughter* by Arthur Guiterman (copyright 1939 by E. P. Dutton and Company, Inc.); and for "Epigram" and "Vista" from *The Selected Poems of Alfred Kreymborg* (copyright 1945 by Alfred Kreymborg); and for "Pretty Polly" from *Bow Down in Jericho* by Byron Herbert Reece (copyright 1950 by Byron Herbert Reece).

Norma Millay Ellis, for "Fatal Interview" from *Collected Sonnets* by Edna St. Vincent Millay; and for "Recuerdo" and "The Spring and the Fall" from *Collected Lyrics of Edna St. Vincent Millay*.

Farrar, Straus and Giroux, Inc., and Faber and Faber Limited, for "The Juniper Tree" from *Friday's Child* by Wilfred Watson (copyright © 1955 by Wilfred Watson).

Lloyd Frankenberg for his poem "The Night of the Full Moon" from *The Red Kite* by Lloyd Frankenberg.

Harcourt, Brace and World, Inc., for "somewhere i have never travelled" from *Poems 1923–1954* by E. E. Cummings (copyright, 1931, 1959, by E. E. Cummings); and for "Silence" from *The Contemplative Quarry and the Man with the Hammer* by Anna Wickham, 1921.

Harvard University Press, for poem #136 "Have you got a brook in your little heart" from *The Poems of Emily Dickinson*, edited by Thomas H. Johnson (Cambridge, Mass.: The Belknap Press of Harvard University; copyright 1951, 1955 by The President and Fellows of Harvard College).

Hill and Wang, Inc., for "Inconsistent," from *Collected and New Poems 1924–1963* by Mark Van Doren (copyright © 1963 by Mark Van Doren).

Holt, Rinehart and Winston, Inc., for "The Walk on the Beach," from *Selected Poems* by John Gould Fletcher (copyright 1938 by John Gould Fletcher); and for "The Rose Family," from *You Come Too* by Robert Frost (copyright 1928 by Holt, Rinehart, and Winston, Inc.; copyright © 1956 by Robert Frost).

Holt, Rinehart and Winston, Inc. and The Society of Authors, representative of the Estate of the late A. E. Housman, and Messrs. Jonathan Cape Limited, publishers of A. E. Housman's *Collected Poems,* for "Oh see how thick the goldcup flowers" and "When I was one-and-twenty" from *A Shropshire Lad—* Authorized Edition—from *The Collected Poems of A. E. Housman* (copyright 1940 by Holt, Rinehart and Winston, Inc.).

Houghton Mifflin Company, for "A Decade" and "Patterns" from *Collected Poems* by Amy Lowell.

The John Day Company, Inc., for "Song" from *Selected Verse* by John Manifold (copyright © 1946 by The John Day Company, Inc.).

Alfred A. Knopf, Inc., for "Parting After a Quarrel" and "Psalm to My

Beloved" from *Body and Raiment* by Eunice Tietjens (copyright 1919 by Alfred
A. Knopf, Inc., renewed, 1947 by Cloyd Head); and for "The Puritan's Ballad"
from *Collected Poems of Elinor Wylie* (copyright 1928 by Alfred A. Knopf, Inc.,
renewed, 1956 by Edwina C. Rubenstein).

Mary Kennedy for her poem "Moon Door."

Sir Geoffrey Keynes, for "The Young Man in April" from *The Poetical Works
of Rupert Brooke*, edited by Sir Geoffrey Keynes.

J. B. Lippincott Company and Hugh Noyes, for "The Highwayman" from
Collected Poems by Alfred Noyes (copyright 1906, 1934 by Alfred Noyes).

Little, Brown and Company—Atlantic Monthly Press, for "A Pavane for the
Nursery" from *Poems 1947–1957* by William Jay Smith (copyright 1954 by
William Jay Smith).

Liveright Publishing Corporation, for "When You're Away" and "Your Little
Hands" from *Poems in Praise of Practically Nothing*, by Samuel Hoffenstein
(copyright © R, 1956 by David Hoffenstein); and for "The Lover Praises His
Lady's Bright Beauty" from *Jealous of Dead Leaves*, by Sheamas O'Sheel (copyright © R, 1956 by Annette K. O'Sheel).

The Macmillan Company, for "The Look" and "Spring Night" from *Collected
Poems* by Sara Teasdale (copyright 1915 by The Macmillan Company, renewed
1943 by Mamie T. Wheless); and for "When I Am Not With You" and "The
Flight" from *Collected Poems* by Sara Teasdale (copyright 1926 by The Macmillan Company, renewed 1954 by Mamie T. Wheless); and for "Pierrot" from
Collected Poems by Sara Teasdale (copyright 1911 by The Macmillan Company); and for "A Deux" from *The Shrinking Orchestra* by William Wood
(copyright © William Wood 1961, 1963).

The Macmillan Company, New York, and the Macmillan Company of Canada
Limited, for "Lines To a Movement in Mozart's E-flat Symphony" from
Collected Poems of Thomas Hardy by permission of the Hardy Estate and
Macmillan and Company Limited, London; and for "Peadar Og Goes Courting"
from *Collected Poems of James Stephens* by permission of Mrs. Iris Wise (copy-
right 1912 by The Macmillan Company, renewed 1940 by James Stephens).

The Macmillan Company, New York and A. P. Watt & Son, and Mrs. W. B.
Yeats, for "Brown Penny" from *Collected Poems* by William Butler Yeats
(copyright 1912 by The Macmillan Company, renewed 1940 by Bertha Georgie
Yeats); and for "Song of Wandering Aengus," "When You Are Old," and
"Down by the Salley Gardens" from *Collected Poems* by William Butler Yeats
(copyright 1906 by The Macmillan Company, renewed 1934 by William Butler
Yeats).

Bob Merrill, for his poem "Promise Me a Rose" from, *Take Me Along*
(copyright © 1958 by Valyr Music Corp.).

The Michigan State University Press, for "Field of Long Grass" from *A
Sort of Ecstasy* by A. J. M. Smith.

Ann Morrissett Davidon for her poem "Here I Am."

Music Publishers Holding Corporation for "Embraceable You" by Ira Gershwin (copyright 1930 by New World Music Corporation, copyright renewed).

New Directions, for "Juliana" from *The Goliard Poets*, Latin originals,
translations and commentary by George F. Whicher (copyright 1949 by George
F. Whicher).

New Directions and Faber and Faber Limited, for "Night Ride" from *Collected Poems* by Herbert Read. All rights reserved.

New Directions and Arthur V. Moore, for "A Girl" and "The River Merchant's Wife: A Letter" from *Personae* by Ezra Pound (copyright 1926, 1954 by Ezra Pound).

Oxford University Press, London, for "After Ever Happily or The Princess and the Woodcutter" from *Happily Ever After* by Ian Serraillier.

Oxford University Press, Inc., New York, for Part I of "Discordants," Part IX from "Improvisations," and Part LVII from "Preludes for Memnon" from *Collected Poems* by Conrad Aiken (copyright 1953 by Conrad Aiken).

A. D. Peters and Company, for "Juliet" and "On a Hand" from *Sonnets and Verse* by Hilaire Belloc.

Random House, Inc., for "The Maid's Thought" from *The Selected Poetry of Robinson Jeffers* (copyright 1924 and renewed 1951 by Robinson Jeffers).

Charles Scribner's Sons, for "Love Comes Quietly" from *For Love* by Robert Creeley (copyright © 1961 by Robert Creeley); and for "As Birds Are Fitted to the Boughs" from *Good News of Death and Other Poems* by Louis Simpson, *Poets of Today II* (copyright 1955 Louis Simpson); and for "I Sought You" and Part III of "Song" from *Poems 1911–1936* by John Hall Wheelock (copyright 1936 Charles Scribner's Sons, renewal copyright © 1964 John Hall Wheelock).

Martin Secker and Warburg Limited and Mrs. Patrick MacDonogh for "She Walked Unaware" from *One Landscape Still* by Patrick MacDonogh.

Shelley Silverstein, for his poem "Mary's eyes are blue as azure."

The University of Chicago Press, for "The Picnic" by John Logan from *Ghosts of the Heart* (copyright © 1960 by The University of Chicago).

The Viking Press, Inc., for "April's Amazing Meaning" from *Boy in the Wind* by George Dillon (copyright 1927 by The Viking Press, Inc., 1955 by George Dillon); and for "Valentine" from *Exiles and Marriages* by Donald Hall (copyright 1955 by Donald Hall); and for "In the dark pine-wood . . ." and "Lean out of the window . . ." from *Collected Poems* by James Joyce (copyright 1918 by B. W. Huebsch, Inc., 1946 by Nora Joyce); and for "Flapper" from *The Complete Poems of D. H. Lawrence,* edited by Vivian de Sola Pinto and F. Warren Roberts (copyright 1920 by B. W. Huebsch, Inc., 1947 by Frieda Lawrence); and for "In a Boat" from *Collected Poems of D. H. Lawrence* (copyright 1929 by Jonathan Cape and Harrison Smith, 1956 by Frieda Lawrence); and for "Spring Morning" from *The Complete Poems of D. H. Lawrence,* edited by Vivian de Sola Pinto and F. Warren Roberts. All rights reserved; and for "The Choice," "Experience," and "Men" from *The Portable Dorothy Parker* (copyright 1926, 1954 by Dorothy Parker).

The Viking Press, Inc. and McClelland and Stewart Limited, for "For Anne" from *The Spice-Box of the Earth* by Leonard Cohen (copyright 1961 by McClelland and Stewart, Limited. All rights reserved.

A. P. Watt and Son, for "Love Without Hope" from *Collected Poems* by Robert Graves, by permission of Hornro N.V., and International Authors N.V.; and for "What is Love?" from *Ballads for Broadbrows* by A. P. Herbert, by permission of Sir Alan Herbert, the Proprietors of *Punch,* and Messrs. Ernest Benn Limited.

To Cambria

Contents

Introduction

Everyone is a poet when he's in love. Love brings out feelings and perceptions we never knew we had; it quickens the senses, it reaches into our deepest emotions. Robert Burns once wrote, "I never had the least thought or inclination of turning poet till I got once heartily in love."

Love is the great changer. It makes strong men weak and weak women strong. The happy lover smiles upon everything and everyone around him. Although his love is directed toward one individual, he finds, to his surprise, that he suddenly likes *every*body. People in love help old women across streets, give money to beggars, and happily dry the dishes. All day, every day, they keep wanting to do good deeds, like eager Boy Scouts. This, of course, is when love goes well; when love is unreturned, or when lovers quarrel, the skies darken, good deeds are forgotten, and all is despair. That too can be a new, strong emotion. To be in love is to feel fully alive, and to find out new things about yourself—which is what poets are always doing.

People in love can be something of a pest; they want to talk about their peculiar condition all the time. Young people in love can be particularly trying; the frequency with which they fall—or plunge—in and out of love seems excessive. And they talk about it—how they talk about it! But they mean it each time; they're testing their wings for the eventual long flight. And they learn something each time they fall in love, however skitterish each time may be, or how short a time it may last. Robert Frost wrote that "A poem begins in delight and ends in wisdom. The figure is the same for love."

But it is foolish to write anything about love in prose when the poets are here to write about it. Anything that man wants to say from the depths of his spirit is a thousand times better expressed in poetry than in prose.

The poems that follow were not chosen because they are all great love poems, but were selected to show the many phases and faces of love. They range from delicate valentines to thundering, breast-thumping declarations; from the frankly cynical and disillusioned to the almost idiotically romantic. Since love isn't always serious, some are jaunty and funny; since love sometimes *is* a matter of life and death, some are genuinely tragic. Their emotions are as varied as the emotions of love itself.

They come in all shapes and sizes, from two lines to a hundred: ballads, sonnets, lyrics, and bits of plays. And songs too: folk songs, music-hall songs, and even two examples of the lyrics of popular songs: Ira Gershwin's neatly-rhymed "Embraceable You" and Bob Merrill's poignant "Promise Me a Rose," which are best heard, of course, with their music, but can stand alone as poetry. The poems are arranged under section headings, mostly to bring out contrasts; it is a pleasant jolt to read a seventeenth-century poet on some aspect of love, followed quickly by a modern poet's views on the same theme, followed by a nineteenth-century poem. It emphasizes love's endless variety to hear from strangely assorted companions—

the magnificence of Shakespeare; the open-collared romantic song of Rupert Brooke; the bitter humor of Samuel Hoffenstein; the quiet sadness of Conrad Aiken; the extremely feminine music of Edna St. Vincent Millay.

This collection of poetry will not teach about love, since there is no teacher of love but love itself; but it will give hints about love's nature and show something of poetry's nature. And that is vitally important. To quote William Hazlitt, the English critic: "He who has a contempt for poetry cannot have much respect for himself or for anything else . . . for all that is worth remembering in life is the poetry of it."

My thanks to four young ladies who gave me their suggestions and reactions: Cambria Cole, Liza Cowan, B. J. Chute, and Joanna Jellinek. And continuing thanks to my increasingly alliterative and valued editor, Velma V. Varner of Viking.

—WILLIAM COLE

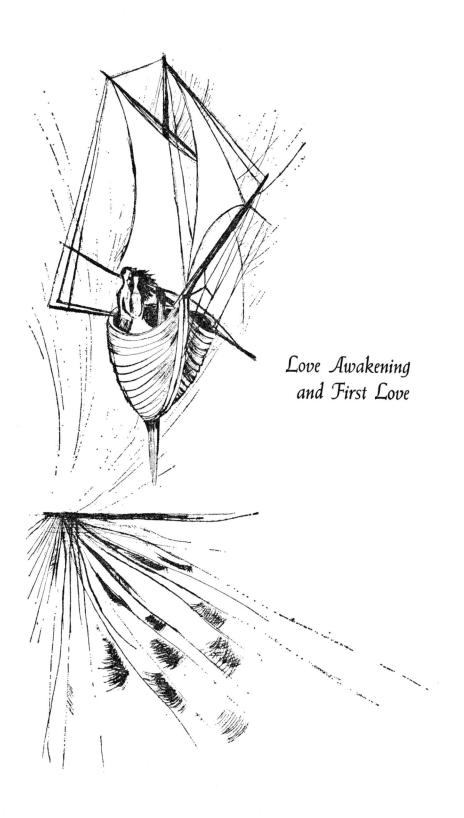

Love Awakening
and First Love

April's Amazing Meaning

April's amazing meaning doubtless lies
    In tall, hoarse boys and slips
of slender girls with suddenly wider eyes
    and parted lips;

For girls must wander pensive in the spring
    When the green rain is over,
Doing some slow, inconsequential thing,
    Plucking clover;

And any boy alone upon a bench
    When his work's done will sit
And stare at the black ground and break a branch
    And whittle it

Slowly; and boys and girls, irresolute,
    Will curse the dreamy weather
Until they meet past the pale hedge and put
    Their lips together.

GEORGE DILLON

Brown Penny

I whispered, "I am too young,"
And then, "I am old enough";
Wherefore I threw a penny
To find out if I might love.
"Go and love, go and love, young man,
If the lady be young and fair."
Ah, penny, brown penny, brown penny,
I am looped in the loops of her hair.
O love is the crooked thing,
There is nobody wise enough
To find out all that is in it,
For he would be thinking of love
Till the stars had run away
And the shadows eaten the moon.
Ah, penny, brown penny, brown penny,
One cannot begin it too soon.

W. B. YEATS

First Flame

Ah, I remember well—and how can I
But ever more remember well—when first
Our flame began, when scarce we knew what was
The flame we felt; when as we sat and sighed,
And looked upon each other, and conceived
Not what we ailed, yet something we did ail,
And yet were well, and yet we were not well,
And what was our disease we could not tell.
Then would we kiss, then sigh, then look: and thus
In that first garden of our simpleness
We spent our childhood: but when years began
To reap the fruit of knowledge, ah, how then

Would she with graver looks, with sweet stern brow,
Check my presumption and my forwardness;
Yet still would give me flowers, still would show
What she would have me, yet not have me, know.

SAMUEL DANIEL

Peadar Og Goes Courting

Now that I am dressed I'll go
Down to where the roses blow,
I'll pluck a fair and fragrant one
And make my mother pin it on:
Now she's laughing, so am I—
Oh the blueness of the sky!

Down the street, turn to the right,
Round the corner out of sight;
Pass the church and out of town—
Dust does show on boots of brown,
I'd better brush them while I can
—Step out, Peadar, be a man!

Here's a field and there's a stile,
Shall I jump it? wait a while,
Scale it gently, stretch a foot
Across the mud in that big rut
And I'm still clean—faith, I'm not!
Get some grass and rub the spot.

Dodge those nettles! Here the stream
Bubbling onward with a gleam
Steely white, and black, and grey,
Bends the rushes on its way—
What's that moving? It's a rat
Washing his whiskers; isn't he fat?

Here the cow with the crumpledy horn
Whisks her tail and looks forlorn,
She wants a milkmaid bad I guess,
How her udders swell and press
Against her legs—And here's some sheep;
And there's the shepherd, fast asleep.

This is a sad and lonely field,
Thistles are all that it can yield;
I'll cross it quick, nor look behind,
There's nothing in it but the wind:
And if those bandy-legged trees
Could talk they'd only curse or sneeze.

A sour, unhappy, sloppy place—
That boot's loose! I'll tie the lace
So, and jump this little ditch,
. . . *Her father's really very rich:*
He'll be angry—There's a crow,
Solemn blackhead! Off you go!

There a big, grey, ancient ass
Is snoozing quiet in the grass;
He hears me coming, starts to rise,
Wags his big ears at the flies:
. . . *What'll I say when*—There's a frog,
Go it, long-legs—jig, jig-jog.

He'll be angry, say—"*Pooh, Pooh,*
Boy, you know not what you do!"
Shakespeare stuff and good advice,
Fat old duffer—Those field mice
Have a good time playing round
Through the corn and underground.

But her mother is friends with mine,
She always asks us out to dine,

And dear Nora, curly head,
Loves me; so at least she said.
. . . Damn that ass's hee-hee-haw—
Was that a rabbit's tail I saw?

This is the house, Lord, I'm afraid!.
A man does suffer for a maid.
. . . *How will I start?* The graining's new
On the door—Oh pluck up, do.
Don't stand shivering there like that.
. . . The knocker's funny—*Rat-tat-tat.*

JAMES STEPHENS

The Maid's Thought

Why listen, even the water is sobbing for something.
The west wind is dead, the waves
Forget to hate the cliff, in the upland canyons
Whole hillsides burst aglow
With golden broom. Dear how it rained last month,
And every pool was rimmed
With sulphury pollen dust of the wakening pines.
Now tall and slender suddenly
The stalks of purple iris blaze by the brooks,
The penciled ones on the hill:
This deerweed shivers with gold, the white globe-tulips
Blow out their silky bubbles,
But in the next glen bronze-bells nod, the does
Scalded by some hot longing
Can hardly set their pointed hoofs to expect
Love but they crush a flower;
Shells pair on the rock, birds mate, the moths fly double.
O it is time for us now
Mouth kindling mouth to entangle our maiden bodies
To make that burning flower.

ROBINSON JEFFERS

21

Young Love

The world is cold and gray and wet,
And I am heavy-hearted, yet
When I am home and look to see
The place my letters wait for me,
If I should find *one* letter there,
I think I should not greatly care
If it were rainy or were fair,
For all the world would suddenly
Seem like a festival to me.

SARA TEASDALE

A Waltz in the Afternoon

A double flower we were
upon a single stem;
my red skirt wrapped our legs
together like a flame
that flared as it was fanned:
the music was our wind.

Snow fell outside the windows.
His lips deep in my hair
dissolved my knee bones; still,
the music was my lover
and loosed my limbs to him.
In innocence we swam.

It was my seventeenth winter.
I saw dances stretch ahead,
an endless scroll brushed lightly,
a hundred waltzes waltzed.
The fiddlers smiled and tapped
their bows; somebody clapped.

Outside, the snow was falling.
His hand firm on my waist
bent and turned and lifted
me. My skirt embraced
our legs. And, in my joy,
I danced childhood away.

It was my seventeenth winter.
No spider on his thread
delighted more in motion.
Sometimes when I'm in bed
I dream that I am swimming
in a calm, a sunny ocean—

it is that dance again.
We swayed the afternoon
away; outside, the snow-
flakes fell. And now I know,
a hundred waltzes after,
that I've not danced since then.

BETH BENTLEY

The Flight

Look back with longing eyes and know that I will follow,
Lift me up in your love as a light wind lifts a swallow,
Let our flight be far in sun or windy rain—
But what if I heard my first love calling me again?

Hold me on your heart as the brave sea holds the foam,
Take me far away to the hills that hide your home;
Peace shall thatch the roof and love shall latch the door—
But what if I heard my first love calling me once more?

SARA TEASDALE

The Young Man in April

In the queer light, in twilight,
    In April of the year,
I meet a thousand women,
    But I never meet my Dear.
Yet each of them has something,
    A turn of neck or knee,
A line of breast or shoulder,
    That brings my Dear to me.

One has a way of swaying,
    I'd swear to anywhere;
One has a laugh, and one a hat,
    And one a trick of hair;
—Oh, glints and hints and gestures,
    When shall I find complete
The Dear that's walking somewhere,
    The Dear I've yet to meet?

RUPERT BROOKE

The Picnic

It is the picnic with Ruth in the spring.
Ruth was third on my list of seven girls
But the first two were gone (Betty) or else
Had someone (Ellen has accepted Doug).
Indian Gully the last day of school;
Girls make the lunches for the boys too.
I wrote a note to Ruth in algebra class
Day before the test. She smiled, and nodded.
We left the cars and walked through the young corn
The shoots green as paint and the leaves like tongues
Trembling. Beyond the fence where we stood

Some wild strawberry flowered by an elm tree
And Jack-in-the-pulpit was olive ripe.
A blackbird fled as I crossed, and showed
A spot of gold or red under its quick wing.
I held the wire for Ruth and watched the whip
Of her long, striped skirt as she followed.
Three freckles blossomed on her thin, white back
Underneath the loop where the blouse buttoned.
We went for our lunch away from the rest,
Stretched in the new grass, our heads close
Over unknown things wrapped up in wax papers.
Ruth tried for the same, I forget what it was,
And our hands were together. She laughed,
And a breeze caught the edge of her little
Collar and the edge of her brown, loose hair
That touched my cheek. I turned my face in-
to the gentle fall. I saw how sweet it smelled.
She didn't move her head or take her hand.
I felt a soft caving in my stomach
As at the top of the highest slide
When I had been a child, but was not afraid,
And did not know why my eyes moved with wet
As I brushed her cheek with my lips and brushed
Her lips with my own lips. She said to me
Jack, Jack, different than I had ever heard,
Because she wasn't calling me, I think,
Or telling me. She used my name to
Talk in another way I wanted to know.
She laughed again and then she took her hand;
I gave her what we both had touched—can't
Remember what it was, and we ate the lunch.
Afterward we walked in the small, cool creek
Our shoes off, her skirt hitched, and she smiling,
My pants rolled, and then we climbed up the high
Side of Indian Gully and looked
Where we had been our hands together again.

It was then some bright thing came in my eyes,
Starting at the back of them and flowing
Suddenly through my head and down my arms
And stomach and my bare legs that seemed not
To stop in feet, not to feel the red earth
Of the gully, as though we hung in a
Touch of birds. There was a word in my throat
With the feeling and I knew the first time
What it meant and I said, it's beautiful.
Yes, she said, and I felt the sound and word
In my hand join the sound and word in hers
As in one name said, or in one cupped hand.
We put back on our shoes and socks and we
Sat in the grass awhile, crosslegged, under
A blowing tree, not saying anything.
And Ruth played with shells she found in the creek,
As I watched. Her small wrist which was so sweet
To me turned by her breast and the shells dropped
Green, white, blue, easily into her lap,
Passing light through themselves. She gave the pale
Shells to me, and got up and touched her hips
With her light hands, and we walked down slowly
To play the school games with the others.

JOHN LOGAN

Conversational

"How's your father?" came the whisper,
    Bashful Ned the silence breaking;
"Oh, he's nicely," Annie murmured,
    Smilingly the question taking.

Conversation flagged a moment,
    Hopeless Ned essayed another:
"Annie, I—I," then a coughing,
    And the question, "How's your mother?"

"Mother? Oh, she's doing finely!"
Fleeting fast was all forbearance,
When in low, despairing accents,
Came the climax, "How's your parents?"

ANONYMOUS

The Garden of Bamboos

I live all alone, and I am a young girl.
I write long letters and do not know anyone to send them to.
Most tender things speak in my heart
And I can only say them to the bamboos in the garden.
Waiting on my feet, lifting the mat a little behind the door,
All day I watch the shadows of the people that pass.

POWYS MATHERS
(Translation of street song of Annam)

Flapper

Love has crept out of her sealèd heart
    As a field-bee, black and amber,
    Breaks from the winter-cell, to clamber
Up the warm grass where the sunbeams start.

Mischief has come in her dawning eyes,
    And a glint of coloured iris brings
    Such as lies along the folded wings
Of the bee before he flies.

Who, with a ruffling, careful breath,
    Has opened the wings of the wild young sprite?
    Has fluttered her spirit to stumbling flight
In her eyes, as a young bee stumbleth?

Love makes the burden of her voice.
　　The hum of his heavy, staggering wings
　　Sets quivering with wisdom the common things
That she says, and her words rejoice.

D. H. LAWRENCE

—Silence —

When I meet you, I greet you with a stare;
Like a poor shy child at a fair.
I will not let you love me, yet am I weak:
I love you so intensely that I cannot speak.
When you are gone, I stand apart
And whisper to your image in my heart.

ANNA WICKHAM

The Brook of the Heart

Have you got a brook in your little heart,
Where bashful flowers blow,
And blushing birds go down to drink,
And shadows tremble so?

And nobody knows, so still it flows,
That any brook is there;
And yet your little draught of life
Is daily drunken there.

Then look out for the little brook in March,
When the rivers overflow,
And the snows come hurrying from the hills,
And the bridges often go.

And *later,* in August it may be,
When the meadows parching lie,
Beware, lest this little brook of life
Some burning noon go dry!

EMILY DICKINSON

Here I Am

Look at me:
I no longer speak French to impress,
Wear innocence on my face by mistake
Or sophisticated sneers on purpose;
I keep my scalp and fingernails clean
And wear whole underwear,
Am not tongue-tied by royalty
Nor do I spit on it.
Workers do not bring tears to my eyes,
But I can talk with them like any other;
I can speak seriously without too much earnestness,
Satirically without too much callousness,
Absurdly without too much foolishness.
I do not envy youth or fear old age,
I can love without butterflies and agony,
But with passion, faithfulness, and good humor.
And now where are you?

ANN MORRISSETT

Spring

Now hand in hand, you little maidens, walk.
Pass in the shadow of the crumbling wall.
Arch your proud bellies under rosy aprons.

And let your eyes so deeply lucid tell
Your joy at feeling flowing into your heart
Another loving heart that blends with yours;
You children faint with being hand in hand.
Walk hand in hand, you langurous maidens, walk.
The boys are turning round, and drinking in
Your sensual petticoats that beat your heels.
And, while you swing your interlacing hands,
Tell, with your warm mouths yearning each to each,
The first books you have read, and your first kisses.
Walk hand in hand, you maidens, friend with friend.

Walk hand in hand, you lovers loving silence.
Walk to the sun that veils itself with willows.
Trail your uneasy limbs by langurous banks,
The stream is full of dusk, your souls are heavy.
You silent lovers, wander hand in hand.

ANDRE SPIRE
(Translated from the French by JETHRO BITHELL)

Longing and Loneliness

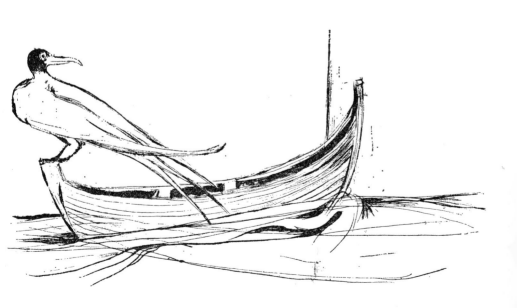

Do You Remember That Night?

Do you remember that night
   That you were at the window,
   With neither hat nor gloves,
   Nor coat to shelter you;
   I reached out my hand to you,
   And you ardently grasped it,
   And I remained in converse with you
   Until the lark began to sing?

Do you remember that night
   That you and I were
   At the foot of the rowan tree,
   And the night drifting snow;
   Your head on my breast,
   And your pipe sweetly playing?
   I little thought that night
   Our ties of love would ever loosen.

O beloved of my inmost heart,
   Come some night, and soon,
   When people are at rest,
   That we may talk together;

My arms shall encircle you,
While I relate my sad tale
That it is your pleasant, soft converse
That has deprived me of heaven.

The fire is unraked,
  The light extinguished,
  The key under the door,
  And do you softly draw it.
  My mother is asleep,
  And I am quite awake;
  My fortune is in my hand,
  And I am ready to go with you.

(Translated from the Gaelic by EUGENE
O'CURRY)

Sonnet XXX

Love is not all: it is not meat nor drink
Nor slumber nor a roof against the rain;
Nor yet a floating spar to men that sink
And rise and sink and rise and sink again;
Love can not fill the thickened lung with breath,
Nor clean the blood, nor set the fractured bone;
Yet many a man is making friends with death
Even as I speak, for lack of love alone.
It well may be that in a difficult hour,
Pinned down by pain and moaning for release,
Or nagged by want past resolution's power,
I might be driven to sell your love for peace,
Or trade the memory of this night for food.
It well may be. I do not think I would.

EDNA ST. VINCENT MILLAY

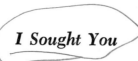

I Sought You

I sought you but I could not find you, all night long
  I called you, but you would not answer—all the night
  I wandered over hill and valley; heaven was bright
With crowded stars, and I was calling you in many a song.

The road through wood and meadow rambled here and there:
  Few were the travellers on that lonely road, and none
  Had heard of you, by wood or meadowland—not one
Had heard of you, or seen you passing anywhere.

At midnight, thirsting for your loveliness, I lay
  Under the shadow of the leafy hill, and cried
  Three times, calling upon your name. No voice replied . . .
The pebbly brooks went babbling, babbling, all the way.

The waters had a drowsy sound, the hills were steep—
  My heart grew tired travelling; but there was no place
  That suited me, and I was homesick for your face.
Dreaming of you, at the wood's edge I fell asleep.

JOHN HALL WHEELOCK

Discordants   CONRAD AIKEN

I

Music I heard with you was more than music,
And bread I broke with you was more than bread;
Now that I am without you, all is desolate;
All that was once so beautiful is dead.

Your hands once touched this table and this silver,
And I have seen your fingers hold this glass.

35

These things do not remember you, belovèd,—
And yet your touch upon them will not pass.

For it was in my heart you moved among them,
And blessed them with your hands and with your eyes;
And in my heart they will remember always,—
They knew you once, O beautiful and wise.

II

My heart has become as hard as a city street,
The horses trample upon it, it sings like iron,
All day long and all night long they beat,
They ring like the hooves of time.

My heart has become as drab as a city park,
The grass is worn with the feet of shameless lovers,
A match is struck, there is kissing in the dark,
The moon comes, pale with sleep.

My heart is torn with the sound of raucous voices,
They shout from the slums, from the streets, from the crowded
        places,
And tunes from a hurdy-gurdy that coldly rejoices
Shoot arrows into my heart.

III

Dead Cleopatra lies in a crystal casket,
Wrapped and spiced by the cunningest of hands.
Around her neck they have put a golden necklace,
Her tatbebs,* it is said, are worn with sands.

Dead Cleopatra was once revered in Egypt,
Warm-eyed she was, this princess of the South.
Now she is very old and dry and faded,
With black bitumen they have sealed up her mouth.

---
* tatbebs: sandals

36

O sweet clean earth, from whom the green blade cometh!
When we are dead, my best belovèd and I,
Close well above us, that we may rest forever,
Sending up grass and blossoms to the sky.

IV

In the noisy street,
Where the sifted sunlight yellows the pallid faces,
Sudden I close my eyes, and on my eyelids
Feel from the far-off sea a cool faint spray,—

A breath on my cheek,
From the tumbling breakers and foam, the hard sand shattered,
Gulls in the high wind whistling, flashing waters,
Smoke from the flashing waters blown on rocks;

—And I know once more,
O dearly belovèd!—that all these seas are between us,
Tumult and madness, desolate save for the sea-gulls,
You on the farther shore, and I in this street.

CONRAD AIKEN

Pining for Love

How long shall I pine for love?
    How long shall I sue in vain?
How long like the turtle-dove,
    Shall I heartily thus complain?
Shall the sails of my heart stand still?
    Shall the grists of my hope be unground?
Oh fie, oh fie, oh fie,
    Let the mill, let the mill go round.

FRANCIS BEAUMONT

Love Without Hope

Love without hope, as when the young bird-catcher
Swept off his tall hat to the Squire's own daughter,
So let the imprisoned larks escape and fly
Singing about her head, as she rode by.

ROBERT GRAVES

 ## Spring Night

The park is filled with night and fog,
   The veils are drawn about the world,
The drowsy lights along the paths
   Are dim and pearled.

Gold and gleaming the empty streets,
   Gold and gleaming the misty lake,
The mirrored lights like sunken swords,
   Glimmer and shake.

Oh, is it not enough to be
Here with this beauty over me?
My throat should ache with praise, and I
Should kneel in joy beneath the sky.
O beauty, are you not enough?
Why am I crying after love
With youth, a singing voice, and eyes
To take earth's wonder with surprise?

Why have I put off my pride,
Why am I unsatisfied,—
I, for whom the pensive night

Renouncement

I must not think of thee; and, tired yet strong,
  I shun the thought that lurks in all delight—
  The thought of thee—and in the blue Heaven's height,
And in the dearest passage of a song.

Oh, just beyond the fairest thoughts that throng
  This breast, the thought of thee waits hidden, yet bright;
  But it must never, never come in sight;
I must stop short of thee the whole day long.

But when sleep comes to close each difficult day,
  When night gives pause to the long watch I keep,
    And all my bonds I needs must loose apart,
Must doff my will as raiment laid away,—
  With the first dream that comes with the first sleep
    I run, I run, I am gathered to thy heart.

ALICE MEYNELL

Juliana

Juliana, one sweet spring,
Stood with her sister, marveling
To see the fruit-trees blossoming.

Sweet love, sweet love!
To miss thee now would be a thing
Past thinking of.

See how bloom bursts from the tree,
And how the birds chant amorously;
So maidens melt in some degree.
Sweet love, sweet love!

See too the lilies, how they flower;
So maidens clustered in a bower
Sing the high god's resistless power:
Sweet love, sweet love!

Could I but hold in close embrace
That girl in some leaf-shadowed place,
Joy! What joy to kiss her face!
Sweet love, sweet love!

GEORGE F. WHICHER
(Translation of Medieval Latin song)

When You're Away

When you're away, I'm restless, lonely,
Wretched, bored, dejected; only
Here's the rub, my darling dear,
I feel the same when you are near.

SAMUEL HOFFENSTEIN

An Apple Gathering

I plucked pink blossoms from mine apple-tree
    And wore them all that evening in my hair:
Then in due season when I went to see
    I found no apples there.

With dangling basket all along the grass
    As I had come I went the selfsame track:
My neighbors mocked me while they saw me pass
    So empty-handed back.

Lilian and Lilias smiled in trudging by,
  Their heaped-up basket teased me like a jeer;
Sweet-voiced they sang beneath the sunset sky,
    Their mother's home was near.

Plump Gertrude passed me with her basket full,
  A stronger hand than hers helped it along;
A voice talked with her through the shadows cool
    More sweet to me than song.

Ah Willie, Willie, was my love less worth
  Than apples with their green leaves piled above?
I counted rosiest apples on the earth
    Of far less worth than love.

So once it was with me you stooped to talk
  Laughing and listening in this very lane;
To think that by this way we used to walk
    We shall not walk again!

I let my neighbors pass me, ones and twos
  And groups; the latest said the night grew chill,
And hastened: but I loitered; while the dews
    Fell fast I loitered still.

CHRISTINA ROSSETTI

I Pass in Silence

I talk to the birds as they sing i' the morn,
The larks and the sparrows that spring from the corn,
The chaffinch and linnet that sing in the bush,
Till the zephyr-like breezes all bid me to hush;
Then silent I go and in fancy I steal

A kiss from the lips of a name I conceal;
But should I meet her I've cherished for years,
I pass by in silence, in fondness and tears.

Yes, I pass her in silence and say not a word,
And the noise of my footsteps may scarcely be heard;
I scarcely presume to cast on her my eye,
And then for a week I do nothing but sigh.
If I look on a wild flower I see her face there;
There it is in its beauty, all radiant and fair;
And should she pass by, I've nothing to say,
We are both of us silent and have our own way.

I talk to the birds, the wind, and the rain;
My love to my dear one I never explain;
I talk to the flowers which are growing all wild,
As if one was herself and the other her child;
I utter sweet words in my fanciful way,
But if she comes by I've nothing to say;
To look for a kiss I would if I dare,
But I feel myself lost when near to my fair.

JOHN CLARE

Indian Serenade

I arise from dreams of thee
In the first sweet sleep of night,
When the winds are breathing low,
And the stars are shining bright;
I arise from dreams of thee,
And a spirit in my feet
Hath led me—who knows how?
To thy chamber window, Sweet!

The wandering airs they faint
On the dark, the silent stream—
The Champak * odors fail
Like sweet thoughts in a dream;
The nightingale's complaint,
It dies upon her heart;—
As I must on thine,
Oh, belovèd as thou art!

Oh, lift me from the grass!
I die! I faint! I fail!
Let thy love in kisses rain
On my lips and eyelids pale.
My cheek is cold and white, alas!
My heart beats loud and fast;—
Oh! press it to thine own again,
Where it will break at last.

PERCY BYSSHE SHELLEY

On a Hand

Her hand which touched my hand she moved away,
But there it lies, for ever and a day.

HILAIRE BELLOC

---

* Champak: East Indian magnolia

45

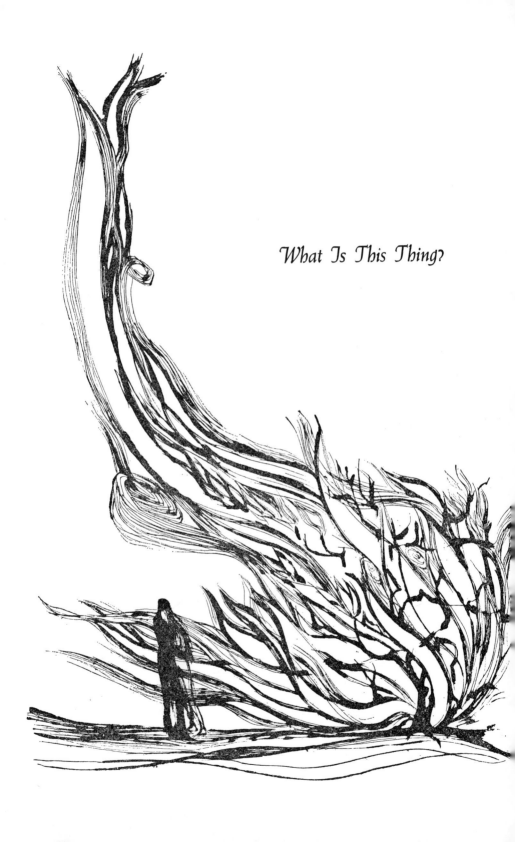

What Is This Thing?

from *Preludes for Memnon*

One star fell and another as we walked.
Lifting his hand toward the west, he said—
—How prodigal that sky is of its stars!
They fall and fall, and still the sky is sky.
Two more have gone, but heaven is heaven still.

Then let us not be precious of our thought,
Nor of our words, nor hoard them up as though
We thought our minds a heaven which might change
And lose its virtue when the word had fallen.
Let us be prodigal, as heaven is;
Lose what we lose, and give what we may give,—
Ourselves are still the same. Lost you a planet—?
Is Saturn gone? Then let him take his rings
Into the Limbo of forgotten things.

O little foplings of the pride of mind,
Who wrap the phrase in lavender, and keep it
In order to display it: and you, who save your loves
As if we had not worlds of love enough—:

Let us be reckless of our words and worlds,
And spend them freely as the trees his leaves;
And give them where the giving is most blest.
What should we save them for,—a night of frost . . . ?
All lost for nothing, and ourselves a ghost.

CONRAD AIKEN

Sonnet CXXX

My mistress' eyes are nothing like the sun;
Coral is far more red than her lips' red:
If snow be white, why then her breasts are dun;
If hairs be wires, black wires grow on her head.
I have seen roses damask'd, red and white,
But no such roses see I in her cheeks;
And in some perfumes is there more delight
Than in the breath that from my mistress reeks.
I love to hear her speak; yet well I know
That music hath a far more pleasing sound:
I grant I never saw a goddess go,
My mistress, when she walks, treads on the ground:
　　And yet, by heaven, I think my love as rare
　　As any she belied with false compare.

WILLIAM SHAKESPEARE

Epigram

Isn't it
that we like each other
quite a little more
than we dislike each other
that we love each other?

ALFRED KREYMBORG

She

I think the dead are tender. Shall we kiss?—
My lady laughs, delighting in what is.
If she but sighs, a bird puts out its tongue.
She makes space lonely with a lovely song.
She lilts a low soft language, and I hear
Down long sea-chambers of the inner ear.

We sing together; we sing mouth to mouth.
The garden is a river flowing south.
She cries out loud the soul's own secret joy;
She dances, and the ground bears her away.
She knows the speech of light, and makes it plain
A lively thing can come to life again.

I feel her presence in the common day,
In that slow dark that widens every eye.
She moves as water moves, and comes to me,
Stayed by what was, and pulled by what would be.

THEODORE ROETHKE

Jealousy

This cursèd jealousy, what is't?
'Tis love that has lost itself in a mist;
'Tis love being frighted out of his wits;
'Tis love that has a fever got;
Love that is violently hot,
But troubled with cold and trembling fits.
'Tis yet a more unnatural evil:
'Tis the god of love . . . possessed with a devil.

'Tis rich corrupted wine of love,
Which sharpest vinegar does prove;
From all the sweet flowers which might honey make,
It does a deadly poison bring:
Strange serpent which itself doth sting! . . .

SIR WILLIAM DAVENANT

Spring Morning

Ah, through the open door
Is there an almond-tree
Aflame with blossom!
   —Let us fight no more.

Among the pink and blue
Of the sky and the almond flowers
A sparrow flutters.
   —We have come through,

It is really spring!—See,
When he thinks himself alone
How he bullies the flowers.
   —Ah, you and me

How happy we'll be!—See him?
He clouts the tufts of flowers
In his impudence
   —But, did you dream

It would be so bitter? Never mind,
It is finished, the spring is here.
And we're going to be summer-happy
   And summer-kind.

We have died, we have slain and been slain,
We are not our old selves any more.
I feel new and eager
   To start again.

It is gorgeous to live and forget.
And to feel quite new.
See the bird in the flowers?—he's making
   A rare to-do!

He thinks the whole blue sky
Is much less than the bit of blue egg
He's got in his nest—we'll be happy,
   You and I, I and you.

With nothing to fight any more—
In each other, at least.
See, how gorgeous the world is
   Outside the door!

D. H. LAWRENCE

When One Loves Tensely   —>

When one loves tensely, words are naught, my Dear!
You never felt I loved you till the day
I sighed and heaved a chunk of rock your way;
Nor I, until you clutched my father's spear
And coyly clipped the lobe from off my ear,
Guessed the sweet thought you were too shy to say—
All mute we listened to the larks of May,
Silent, we harked the laughter of the year.

Later, my Dear, I'll say you spoke enough!
Do you remember how I took you, Sweet,
And banged your head upon the frozen rill
Until I broke the ice, and by your feet
Held you submerged until your tongue was still?
When one loves tensely, one is sometimes rough.

DON MARQUIS

from *What Is Love?*

"What is Love?" the poets question,
     And their answers don't impress;
But if they have no suggestion
     You and I can give a guess.
What is Love, that makes us gay
In this idiotic way?
Well, I'll whisper if I may—
     What is Love?
          A perfect nuisance.

What is Love? It's Nature's blunder.
     What is Love? A waste of time.
What is Love? A nine days' wonder.
     What is Love? The cause of crime.
          What is Lo-o-o-o-ove?
          What is Lo-o-o-o-ove?
What is Love? A perfect nuisance—
     But I love you.

What is Love, that, swift or slowly,
     Brings all mortals to their knees?
Is it horrid? Is it holy?
     Is it some obscure disease?

What is Love, that, Jew or Turk,
Lord or lackey, makes us shirk
Duty, Family and Work?
    What is Love?
    A public nuisance.

What is Love? A kind of measles.
What is Love? The end of sense.
What is Love? The cause of weasels.
What is Love? A great expense.
What is Lo-o-o-o-ove?
What is Lo-o-o-o-ove?
What is Love? A certain loser—
But I love you.

A. P. HERBERT

Love Poem

When we are in love, we love the grass,
And the barns, and the lightpoles,
And the small mainstreets abandoned all night.

ROBERT BLY

A Proverb

Before you love,
Learn to run through snow
Leaving no footprint.

POWYS MATHERS
(Translated from the Turkish)

Let Her Give Her Hand

Let her give her hand, her glove;
Let her sigh and swear she dies;
He that thinks he hath her love,
I shall never think him wise:
  For be the old love ne'er so true,
  She is ever for the new.

One nail drives another forth;
Land must lose where sea doth win;
Last that comes, though least of worth,
Drives him out that first was in:
  So be the old love ne'er so true
  She is ever for the new.

Store of dishes makes the feast;
Shift of clothes is sweet and clean;
Change of pasture fats the beast,
Think you then she will be lean?
  For be the old love ne'er so true,
  She is ever for the new.

ANONYMOUS

The Passionate Shepherd to His Love

Come live with me, and be my love,
And we will all the pleasures prove,
That valleys, groves, hills and fields,
Woods, or steepy mountains yields.

And we will sit upon the rocks,
Seeing the shepherds feed their flocks,
By shallow rivers, to whose falls,
Melodious birds sing madrigals.

And I will make thee beds of roses,
And a thousand fragrant posies,
A cap of flowers, and a kirtle
Embroidered all with leaves of myrtle;

A gown made of the finest wool,
Which from our pretty lambs we pull,
Fair lined slippers for the cold,
With buckles of the purest gold;

A belt of straw and ivy buds
With coral clasps and amber studs:
And if these pleasures may thee move,
Come live with me, and be my love.

The shepherd swains shall dance and sing,
For thy delight each May morning:
If these delights thy mind may move,
Then live with me, and be my love.

CHRISTOPHER MARLOWE

Shall I, Wasting in Despair

Shall I, wasting in despair,
Die because a woman's fair?
Or make pale my cheeks with care
'Cause another's rosy are?
Be she fairer than the day,
Or the flowery meads in May,
    If she think not well of me,
    What care I how fair she be?

Should my heart be grieved or pined
'Cause I see a woman kind?

Or a well-disposèd nature
Joinèd with a lovely feature?
Be she meeker, kinder than
Turtle-dove, or pelican,
    If she be not so to me,
    What care I how kind she be?

Shall a woman's virtues move
Me to perish for her love?
Or her well-deservings known,
Make me quite forget mine own?
Be she with that goodness blessed
Which may merit name of Best,
    If she be not such to me,
    What care I how good she be?

Great or good, or kind, or fair,
I shall ne'er the more despair;
If she love me, this believe,
I will die ere she shall grieve;
If she slight me when I woo,
I can scorn and let her go;
    For if she be not for me,
    What care I for whom she be?

GEORGE WITHER

A Modest Love

The lowest trees have tops, the ant her gall,
    The fly her spleen, the little sparks their heat;
The slender hairs cast shadows, though but small,
    And bees have stings, although they be not great;
Seas have their source, and so have shallow springs;
And love is love, in beggars as in kings.

Where rivers smoothest run, deep are the fords;
   The dial stirs, yet none perceives it move;
The firmest faith is in the fewest words;
   The turtles cannot sing, and yet they love:
True hearts have eyes and ears, no tongues to speak;
They hear and see, and sigh and then they break.

SIR EDWARD DYER

Juliet

How did the party go in Portman Square?
I cannot tell you; Juliet was not there.

And how did Lady Gaster's party go?
Juliet was next me and I do not know.

HILAIRE BELLOC

Oblation

Ask nothing more of me, sweet;
   All I can give you I give;
   Heart of my heart, were it more,
More should be laid at your feet:
   Love that should help you to live,—
   Song that should spur you to soar.

All things were nothing to give,
   Once to have sense of you more,—
   Touch you and taste of you, sweet,
Think you and breathe you, and live
   Swept of your wings as they soar,
   Trodden by chance of your feet.

I, who have love and no more,
   Bring you but love of you, sweet.
      He that hath more, let him give;
He that hath wings, let him soar:
   Mine is the heart at your feet
      Here, that must love you to live.

ALGERNON CHARLES SWINBURNE

Vista

The snow,
ah yes, ah yes indeed,
is white and beautiful, white and beautiful,
verily beautiful—
from my window.
The sea,
ah yes, ah yes indeed,
is green and alluring, green and alluring,
verily alluring—
from the shore.
Love?—
ah yes, ah yes, ah yes indeed,
verily yes, ah yes indeed!

ALFRED KREYMBORG

Sonnet LVII

Being your slave, what should I do but tend
Upon the hours and times of your desire?
I have no precious time at all to spend,
Nor services to do, till you require.
Nor dare I chide the world-without-end hour

Whilst I, my sovereign, watch the clock for you,
Nor think the bitterness of absence sour
When you have bid your servant once adieu;
Nor dare I question with my jealous thought
Where you may be, or your affairs suppose,
But, like a sad slave, stay and think of nought
Save, where you are how happy you make those.
  So true a fool is love that in your will,
  Though you do any thing, he thinks no ill.

WILLIAM SHAKESPEARE

Mary's eyes are blue as azure,
But she is in love with Freddy;
Sue is sweet but Ronald has her,
Lovely Joan is going steady.
Helen hates me, so does May,
Eloise will not be mine;
Barbara lives too far away—
Will you be my valentine?

SHEL SILVERSTEIN

When I Was One-and-Twenty

When I was one-and-twenty
  I heard a wise man say,
"Give crowns and pounds and guineas
  But not your heart away;
Give pearls away and rubies
  But keep your fancy free."
But I was one-and-twenty,
  No use to talk to me.

When I was one-and-twenty
  I heard him say again,
"The heart out of the bosom
  Was never given in vain;
'Tis paid with sighs a plenty
  And sold for endless rue."
And I am two-and-twenty,
  And oh, 'tis true, 'tis true.

A. E. HOUSMAN

Love is like a lamb, and love is like a lion;
Fly from love, he fights; fight, then does he fly on;
Love is all in fire, and yet is ever freezing;
Love is much in winning, yet is more in leezing;*
Love is ever sick, and yet is never dying;
Love is ever true, and yet is ever lying;
Love does dote in liking, and is mad in loathing;
Love indeed is anything, yet indeed is nothing.

THOMAS MIDDLETON

A Deux

I twist your arm,
You twist my leg,
I make you cry,
You make me beg,
I dry your eyes,
You wipe my nose,
And that's the way
The Loving goes.

WILLIAM WOOD

* leezing: losing

62

from *Two in the Campagna*

How say you? Let us, O my dove,
   Let us be unashamed of soul,
As earth lies bare to heaven above!
   How is it under our control
To love or not to love?

I would that you were all to me,
   You that are just so much, no more.
Nor yours nor mine, nor slave nor free!
   Where does the fault lie? What the core
O' the wound, since wound must be?

I would I could adopt your will,
   See with your eyes, and set my heart
Beating by yours, and drink my fill
   At your soul's springs,—your part my part
In life, for good and ill.

                  ROBERT BROWNING

The Time I've Lost in Wooing

The time I've lost in wooing
In watching and pursuing
   The light that lies
   In woman's eyes,
Has been my heart's undoing.
Though Wisdom oft has sought me,
I scorned the lore she brought me,
   My only books
   Were woman's looks,
And folly's all they've taught me.

Her smile when Beauty granted,
I hung with gaze enchanted,
 Like him the Sprite,
  Whom maids by night
Oft meet in glen that's haunted.
Like him, too, Beauty won me,
But while her eyes were on me,
 If once their ray
  Was turned away,
O, winds could not outrun me.

And are those follies going?
And is my proud heart growing
 Too cold or wise
  For brilliant eyes
Again to set it glowing?
No, vain, alas! th' endeavor
From bonds so sweet to sever;—
 Poor Wisdom's chance
  Against a glance
Is now as weak as ever.

THOMAS MOORE

Song

So, we'll go no more a-roving
 So late into the night,
Though the heart be still as loving,
 And the moon be still as bright.

For the sword outwears its sheath,
 And the soul wears out the breast,
And the heart must pause to breathe,
 And love itself have rest.

Though the night was made for loving,
  And the day returns too soon,
Yet we'll go no more a-roving
  By the light of the moon.

GEORGE GORDON, LORD BYRON

He Writes
about Her

Song

Nay but you, who do not love her,
  Is she not pure gold, my mistress?
Holds earth aught—speak truth—above her?
  Aught like this tress, see, and this tress,
And this last fairest tress of all,
So fair, see, ere I let it fall?

Because, you spend your lives in praising;
  To praise, you search the wide world over:
Then why not witness, calmly gazing,
  If earth holds aught—speak truth—above her?
Above this tress, and this, I touch
But cannot praise, I love so much!

ROBERT BROWNING

69

The Lover Praises His Lady's Bright Beauty

Some night I think if you should walk with me
Where the tall trees like ferns on the ocean's floor
Sway slowly in the blue deeps of the moon's flood,
I would put up my hands through that impalpable sea
And tear a branch of stars from the sky, as once I tore
A branch of apple blossoms for you in an April wood.

And I would bend the dewy branch of stars about your little
    head
Till they flamed with pride to be as blossoms amid your hair,
But I would laugh to see them so pale, being near your eyes.
I would say to you, "Love, the Immortals are hovering about
    your head,
They laugh at the dimness of stars in the luminous night of
    your hair."
I would toss that weeping branch back to the mournful skies.

SHAEMAS O'SHEEL

A Girl

The tree has entered my hands,
The sap has ascended my arms,
The tree has grown in my breast—
Downward,
The branches grow out of me, like arms.

Tree you are,
Moss you are,
You are violets with wind above them.
A child—so high—you are,
And all this folly to the world.

EZRA POUND

Who Is Silvia?

Who is Silvia? What is she,
  That all our swains commend her?
Holy, fair, and wise is she:
  The heavens such grace did lend her,
That she might admired be.

Is she kind as she is fair?
  For beauty lives with kindness.
Love doth to her eyes repair
  To help him of his blindness,
And, being helped, inhabits there.

Then to Silvia let us sing,
  That Silvia is excelling;
She excels each mortal thing
  Upon the dull earth dwelling:
To her let us garlands bring.

WILLIAM SHAKESPEARE

Field of Long Grass

When she walks in the field of long grass
The delicate little hands of the grass
Lean forward a little to touch her.

Light is like the waving of the long grass.
Light is the faint to and fro of her dress.
Light rests for a while in her bosom.

When it is all gone from her bosom's hollow
And out of the field of long grass,
She walks in the dark by the edge of the fallow land.

Then she begins to walk in my heart.
Then she walks in me, swaying in my veins.

My wrists are a field of long grass
A little wind is kissing.

A. J. M. SMITH

Mexican Serenade

When the little armadillo
With his head upon the pillow
   Sweetly rests,
And the parrakeet and lindo
Flitting past my cabin window
   Seek their nests,—

When the mists of evening settle
Over Popocatapetl,
   Dropping dew,—
Like the condor, brooding yonder,
Still I ponder, ever fonder
   Dear, of you!

May no revolution shock you,
May the earthquake gently rock you
   To repose,
While the sentimental panthers
Sniff the pollen-laden anthers
   Of the rose.

While the pelican is pining,
While the moon is softly shining
   On the stream,
May the song that I am singing
Send a tender cadence ringing
   Through your dream.

I have just one wish to utter,
That you twinkle through your shutter
    Like a star,
While, according to convention,
I melodiously mention
    My guitar.

Senorita Maraquita,
Muy chiquita y bonita,
    Hear my lay!
But the dew is growing wetter
And perhaps you think I'd better
    Fade away.

ARTHUR GUITERMAN

To Phillis

Phillis is my only joy,
    Faithless as the winds or seas,
Sometimes cunning, sometimes coy,
    Yet she never fails to please:
        If with a frown
        I am cast down,
        Phillis, smiling
        And beguiling,
Makes me happier than before.

Though alas! too late I find
    Nothing can her fancy fix;
Yet the moment she is kind
    I forgive her with her tricks,
        Which though I see
        I can't get free:
        She deceiving,
        I believing,
What need lovers wish for more?

SIR CHARLES SEDLEY

As Birds Are Fitted to the Boughs

As birds are fitted to the boughs
That blossom on the tree
And whisper when the south wind blows—
So was my love to me.

And still she blossoms in my mind
And whispers softly, though
The clouds are fitted to the wind,
The wind is to the snow.

LOUIS SIMPSON

Inconsistent

Let no man see my girl;
Let all see, and admire.
Why do I contradict
Myself? Do not inquire.

MARK VAN DOREN

from *Come into the Garden, Maud*

Come into the garden, Maud,
  For the black bat, night, has flown,
Come into the garden, Maud,

  I am here at the gate alone;
And the woodbine spices are wafted abroad,
  And the musk of the rose is blown.

For a breeze of morning moves,
  And the planet of Love is on high,

Beginning to faint in the light that she loves
  On a bed of daffodil sky,
To faint in the light of the sun she loves,
  To faint in his light, and to die.

All night have the roses heard
  The flute, violin, bassoon;
All night has the casement jessamine stirred
  To the dancers dancing in tune;
Till a silence fell with the waking bird,
  And a hush with the setting moon.

*   *   *

Queen rose of the rosebud garden of girls,
  Come hither, the dances are done,
In gloss of satin and glimmer of pearls,
  Queen lily and rose in one;
Shine out, little head, sunning over with curls,
  To the flowers, and be their sun.

There has fallen a splendid tear
  From the passion-flower at the gate.
She is coming, my dove, my dear;
  She is coming, my life, my fate;
The red rose cries, "She is near, she is near";
  And the white rose weeps, "She is late";
The larkspur listens, "I hear, I hear";
  And the lily whispers, "I wait".

She is coming, my own, my sweet;
  Were it ever so airy a tread,
My heart would hear her and beat,
  Were it earth in an earthy bed;

My dust would hear her and beat,
  Had I lain for a century dead;

Would start and tremble under her feet,
And blossom in purple and red.

ALFRED, LORD TENNYSON

To Helen

Helen, thy beauty is to me
   Like those Nicéan barks of yore,
That gently, o'er a perfumed sea,
   The weary, way-worn wanderer bore
To his own native shore.

On desperate seas long wont to roam,
   Thy hyacinth hair, thy classic face,
Thy Naiad airs have brought me home
   To the glory that was Greece,
And the grandeur that was Rome.

Lo! in yon brilliant window-niche
   How statue-like I see thee stand,
   The agate lamp within thy hand!
Ah, Psyche, from the regions which
   Are Holy Land!

EDGAR ALLAN POE

somewhere i have never travelled,gladly beyond
any experience, your eyes have their silence:
in your most frail gesture are things which enclose me,
or which i cannot touch because they are too near

your slightest look easily will unclose me
though i have closed myself as fingers,

you open always petal by petal myself as Spring opens
(touching skilfully,mysteriously)her first rose

or if your wish be to close me,i and
my life will shut very beautifully,suddenly,
as when the heart of this flower imagines
the snow carefully everywhere descending;

nothing which we are to perceive in this world equals
the power of your intense fragility:whose texture
compels me with the colour of its countries,
rendering death and forever with each breathing

(i do not know what it is about you that closes
and opens;only something in me understands
the voice of your eyes is deeper than all roses)
nobody,not even the rain,has such small hands

E. E. CUMMINGS

To His Mistress

My light thou art, without thy glorious sight
My eyes are darkened with eternal night;
My love, thou art my way, my life, my light.

Thou art my way, I wander if thou fly;
Thou art my light, if hid, how blind am I!
Thou art my life, if thou withdraw'st I die.

Thou art my life, if thou but turn away,
My life's a thousand deaths. Thou art my way;
Without thee, love, I travel not, but stray.

JOHN WILMOT, EARL OF ROCHESTER

Out upon it, I have loved
  Three whole days together;
And am I like to love three more,
  If it prove fair weather.

Time shall moult away his wings
  Ere he shall discover
In the whole wide world again
  Such a constant Lover.

But the spite on't is, no praise
  Is due at all to me:
Love with me had made no stays
  Had it any been but she.

Had it any been but she
  And that very Face,
There had been at least ere this
  A dozen dozen in her place.

                    SIR JOHN SUCKLING

Amo Amas

Amo, Amas, I love a lass
As a cedar tall and slender;
Sweet cowslip's grace is her nominative case,
And she's of the feminine gender.

  Rorum, Corum, sunt divorum,
  Harum, Scarum divo;
  Tag-rag, merry-derry, periwig and hat-band
  Hic hoc horum genitivo.

Can I decline a Nymph divine?
Her voice as a flute is dulcis.

Her oculus bright, her manus white,
And soft, when I tacto, her pulse is.

Rorum, Corum, sunt divorum,
Harum, Scarum divo;
Tag-rag, merry-derry, periwig and hat-band
Hic hoc horum genitivo.

Oh, how bella my puella,
I'll kiss secula seculorum.
If I've luck, sir, she's my uxor,
O dies benedictorum.

Rorum, Corum, sunt divorum,
Harum, Scarum divo;
Tag-rag, merry-derry, periwig and hat-band
Hic hoc horum genitivo.

JOHN O'KEEFE

There Is a Lady . . .

There is a lady sweet and kind,
Was never face so pleased my mind;
I did but see her passing by,
And yet I love her till I die.

Her gesture, motion, and her smiles,
Her wit, her voice, my heart beguiles,
Beguiles my heart, I know not why,
And yet I love her till I die.

Her free behavior, winning looks,
Will make a lawyer burn his books;
I touched her not, alas! not I,
And yet I love her till I die.

Had I her fast betwixt mine arms,
Judge you that think such sports were harms,
Were't any harm? no, no, fie, fie,
For I will love her till I die.

Should I remain confinèd there
So long as Phoebus in his sphere,
I to request, she to deny,
Yet would I love her till I die.

Cupid is wingèd and doth range,
Her country so my love doth change:
But change she earth, or change she sky,
Yet will I love her till I die.

ANONYMOUS

When You Are Old

When you are old and grey and full of sleep,
And nodding by the fire, take down this book,
And slowly read, and dream of the soft look
Your eyes had once, and of their shadows deep;

How many loved your moments of glad grace,
And loved your beauty with love false or true,
But one man loved the pilgrim soul in you,
And loved the sorrows of your changing face;

And bending down beside the glowing bars,
Murmur, a little sadly, how Love fled
And paced upon the mountains overhead
And hid his face amid a crowd of stars.

W. B. YEATS

Love in the Winds

When I am standing on a mountain crest,
Or hold the tiller in the dashing spray,
My love of you leaps foaming in my breast,
Shouts with the winds and sweeps to their foray;
My heart bounds with the horses of the sea,
And plunges in the wild ride of the night,
Flaunts in the teeth of tempest the large glee
That rides our Fate and welcomes gods to fight.
Ho, love, I laugh aloud for love of you,
Glad that our love is fellow to rough weather,—
No fretful orchid hothoused from the dew,
But hale and hardy as the highland heather,
Rejoicing in the wind that stings and thrills,
Comrade of ocean, playmate of the hills.

RICHARD HOVEY

To His Mistress

There comes an end to summer,
    To spring showers and hoar rime;
His mumming to each mummer
    Has somewhere end in time,
And since life ends and laughter,
    And leaves fall and tears dry,
Who shall call love immortal,
    When all that is must die?

Nay, sweet, let's leave unspoken
    The vows the fates gainsay,
For all vows made are broken,
    We love but while we may.

Let's kiss when kissing pleases,
  And part when kisses pall,
Perchance, this time to-morrow,
  We shall not love at all.

You ask my love completest,
  As strong next year as now,
The devil take you, sweetest,
  Ere I make aught such vow.
Life is a masque that changes,
  A fig for constancy!
No love at all were better,
  Than love which is not free.

ERNEST DOWSON

Love on the Mountain

My love comes down from the mountain
  Through the mists of dawn;
I look, and the star of the morning
  From the sky is gone.

My love comes down from the mountain,
  At dawn, dewy-sweet;
Did you step from the star to the mountain,
  O little white feet?

O whence came your twining tresses
  And your shining eyes,
But out of the gold of the morning
  And the blue of the skies?

The misty mountain is burning
  In the sun's red fire,

And the heart in my breast is burning
And lost in desire.

I follow you into the valley
But no word can I say;
To the East or the West I will follow
Till the dusk of my day.

THOMAS BOYD

The Rose Family

The rose is a rose,
And was always a rose.
But the theory now goes
That the apple's a rose,
And the pear is, and so's
The plum, I suppose.
The dear only knows
What will next prove a rose—
You, of course, are a rose—
But were always a rose.

ROBERT FROST

A Red, Red Rose

O My Luve's like a red, red rose,
That's newly sprung in June.
O my Luve's like the melodie
That's sweetly play'd in tune.

As fair art thou my bonnie lass,
So deep in luve am I;

And I will love thee still, my Dear,
   Till a' the seas gang * dry.

Till a' the seas gang dry, my Dear,
   And the rocks melt wi' the sun:
I will love thee still, my Dear,
   While the sands o' life shall run:

And fare thee weel, my only Luve!
   And fare thee weel, a while!
And I will come again, my Luve,
   Tho' it ware ten thousand mile!

ROBERT BURNS

Dover Beach

The sea is calm to-night.
The tide is full, the moon lies fair
Upon the straits;—on the French coast the light
Gleams and is gone; the cliffs of England stand,
Glimmering and vast, out in the tranquil bay.
Come to the window, sweet is the night-air!
Only, from the long line of spray
Where the sea meets the moon-blanch'd land,
Listen! you hear the grating roar
Of pebbles which the waves draw back, and fling,
At their return, up the high strand,
Begin, and cease, and then again begin,
With tremulous cadence slow, and bring
The eternal note of sadness in.

Sophocles long ago
Heard it on the Aegaean, and it brought
Into his mind the turbid ebb and flow

---

* gang: go

Of human misery; we
Find also in the sound a thought,
Hearing it by this distant northern sea.

The Sea of Faith
Was once, too, at the full, and round earth's shore
Lay like the folds of a bright girdle furl'd.
But now I only hear
Its melancholy, long, withdrawing roar,
Retreating, to the breath
Of the night-wind, down the vast edges drear
And naked shingles of the world.

Ah, love, let us be true
To one another! for the world, which seems
To lie before us like a land of dreams,
So various, so beautiful, so new,
Hath really neither joy, nor love, nor light,
Nor certitude, nor peace, nor help for pain;
And we are here as on a darkling plain
Swept with confused alarms of struggle and flight,
Where ignorant armies clash by night.

MATTHEW ARNOLD

Come Hither, My Dear One

Come hither, my dear one, my choice one, and rare one,
    And let us be walking the meadows so fair,
Where on pilewort and daisies the eye fondly gazes,
    And the wind plays so sweet in thy bonny brown hair.

Come with thy maiden eye, lay silks and satins by;
    Come in thy russet or grey cotton gown;

Come to the meads, dear, where flags, sedge, and reeds appear,
  Rustling to soft winds and bowing low down.

Come with thy parted hair, bright eyes, and forehead bare;
  Come to the whitethorn that grows in the lane;
To banks of primroses, where sweetness reposes,
  Come, love, and let us be happy again.

Come where the violet flowers, come where the morning
    showers
  Pearl on the primrose and speedwell so blue;
Come to that clearest brook that ever runs round the nook
  Where you and I pledged our first love so true.

JOHN CLARE

Lines supposed to have been addressed to Fanny Brawne

This living hand, now warm and capable
Of earnest grasping, would, if it were cold
And in the icy silence of the tomb,
So haunt thy days and chill thy dreaming nights
That thou wouldst wish thine own heart dry of blood
So in my veins red life might stream again,
And thou be conscience-calm'd—see here it is—
I hold it towards you.

JOHN KEATS

Lean out of the window,
  Goldenhair,
I heard you singing
  A merry air.

My book was closed;
   I read no more,
Watching the fire dance
   On the floor.

I have left my book,
   I have left my room,
For I heard you singing
   Through the gloom.

Singing and singing
   A merry air,
Lean out of the window,
   Goldenhair.

JAMES JOYCE

Song

My dark-headed Käthchen, my spit-kitten darling,
You stick in my mind like an arrow of barley;
You stick in my mind like a burr on a bear,
And you drive me distracted by not being here.

I think of you singing when dullards are talking,
I think of you fighting when fools are provoking;
To think of you now makes me faint on my feet,
And you tear me to pieces by being so sweet.

The heart in my chest like a colt in a noose
Goes plunging and straining, but it's no bloody use;
It's no bloody use, but you stick in my mind,
And tear me to pieces by being so kind.

JOHN MANIFOLD

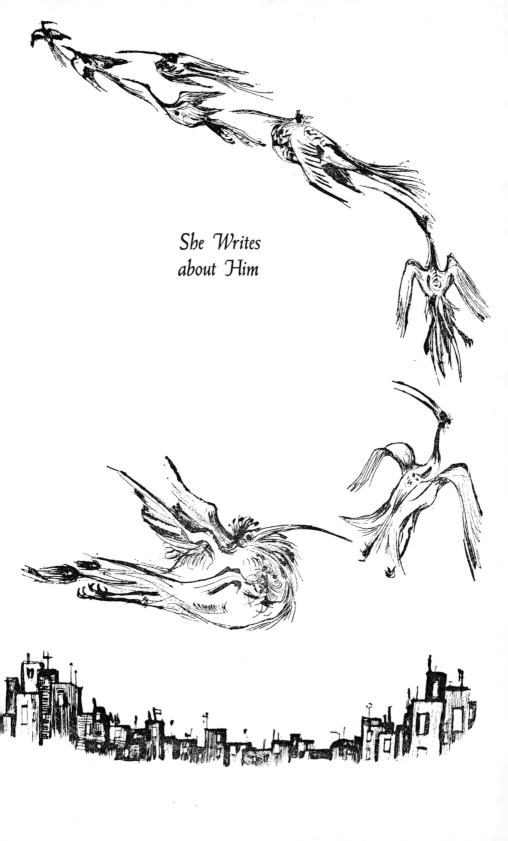

*She Writes
about Him*

The Look

Strephon kissed me in the spring,
    Robin in the fall,
But Colin only looked at me
    And never kissed at all.

Strephon's kiss was lost in jest,
    Robin's lost in play,
But the kiss in Colin's eyes
    Haunts me night and day.

                SARA TEASDALE

How do I love thee? Let me count the ways.
I love thee to the depth and breadth and height
My soul can reach, when feeling out of sight
For the ends of Being and ideal Grace.
I love thee to the level of every day's
Most quiet need, by sun and candle-light.
I love thee freely, as men strive for right;
I love thee purely, as they turn from praise.
I love thee with the passion put to use
In my old griefs, and with my childhood's faith.
I love thee with a love I seemed to lose
With my lost saints—I love thee with the breath,
Smiles, tears, of all my life!—and, if God choose,
I shall but love thee better after death.

        ELIZABETH BARRETT BROWNING

The Puritan's Ballad

My love came up from Barnegat,
  The sea was in his eyes;
He trod as softly as a cat
  And told me terrible lies.

His hair was yellow as new-cut pine
  In shavings curled and feathered;
I thought how silver it would shine
  By cruel winters weathered.

But he was in his twentieth year,
  This time I'm speaking of;
We were head over heels in love with fear
  And half a-feared of love.

His feet were used to treading a gale
  And balancing thereon;
His face was brown as a foreign sail
  Threadbare against the sun.

His arms were thick as hickory logs
  Whittled to little wrists;
Strong as the teeth of terrier dogs
  Were the fingers of his fists.

Within his arms I feared to sink
  Where lions shook their manes,
And dragons drawn in azure ink
  Leapt quickened by his veins.

Dreadful his strength and length of limb
  As the sea to foundering ships;
I dipped my hands in love for him
  No deeper than their tips.

But our palms were welded by a flame
   The moment we came to part,
And on his knuckles I read my name
   Enscrolled within a heart.

And something made our wills to bend
   As wild as trees blown over;
We were no longer friend and friend,
   But only lover and lover.

"In seven weeks or seventy years—
   God grant it may be sooner!—
I'll make a handkerchief for your tears
   From the sails of my captain's schooner.

"We'll wear our loves like wedding rings
   Long polished to our touch;
We shall be busy with other things
   And they cannot bother us much.

"When you are skimming the wrinkled cream
   And your ring clinks on the pan,
You'll say to yourself in a pensive dream,
   'How wonderful a man!'

"When I am slitting a fish's head
   And my ring clanks on the knife,
I'll say with thanks, as a prayer is said,
   'How beautiful a wife!'

"And I shall fold my decorous paws
   In velvet smooth and deep,
Like a kitten that covers up its claws
   To sleep and sleep and sleep.

"Like a little blue pigeon you shall bow
    Your bright alarming crest;
In the crook of my arm you'll lay your brow
    To rest and rest and rest."

Will he never come back from Barnegat
    With thunder in his eyes,
Treading as soft as a tiger cat,
    To tell me terrible lies?

ELINOR WYLIE

A Girl

I don't know any more what it used to be
Before I saw you at table sitting across from me
All I remember is I saw you look at me
And I couldn't breathe and I hurt so bad I couldn't see.

I couldn't see but just your looking eyes
And my ears was buzzing with a thumping noise
And I was scared the way everything went rushing around
Like I was all alone, like I was going to drown.

There wasn't nothin left except the light of your face
There might have been no people, there might have been no
    place
Like as if a dream were to be stronger than thought
And could walk into the sun and be stronger than aught.

Then someone says somethin and then you spoke
And I couldn't hardly answer up, but it sounded like a croak
So I just sat still and nobody knew
That since that happened all of everything is you.

EDWIN DENBY

94

The Jilted Nymph

I'm jilted, forsaken, outwitted;
   Yet think not I'll whimper or brawl—
The lass is alone to be pitied
   Who ne'er has been courted at all:
Never by great or small,
Woo'd or jilted at all;
   Oh, how unhappy's the lass
Who has never been courted at all!

What though at my heart he has tilted,
   What though I have met with a fall?
Better be courted and jilted
   Than never be courted at all.
Woo'd and jilted and all,
Still I will dance at the ball;
   And waltz and quadrille
   With light heart and heel,
With proper young men and tall.

THOMAS CAMPBELL

The Choice

He'd have given me rolling lands,
   Houses of marble, and billowing farms,
Pearls, to trickle between my hands,
   Smoldering rubies, to circle my arms,
You—you'd only a lilting song,
   Only a melody, happy and high,
You were sudden and swift and strong—
   Never a thought for another had I.

He'd have given me laces rare,
   Dresses that glimmered with frosty sheen,

95

Shining ribbons to wrap my hair,
  Horses to draw me, as fine as a queen.
You—you'd only to whistle low,
  Gayly I followed wherever you led.
I took you, and I let him go—
  Somebody ought to examine my head!

DOROTHY PARKER

Promise Me a Rose

(from the musical "Take Me Along")

If you promise me a rose,
  I go out and buy a pot;
My imagination grows
  Into roses by the plot.
I have roses on the doors,
  On my ceiling and my floors—
And if you forget to keep your promise,
  For some reason or another you fail;
How can a dreamer of such sweet roses
  Be bothered by a slight detail?

If you promise me a bird,
  One to sing above my chair;
Then a dream in me is stirred,
  And one bird becomes a pair.
Then my room is full of song,
  'Cause the pair become a throng—

And if you forget to keep your promise,
  For some reason or another you fail;
How can a dreamer of such sweet music
  Be bothered by a slight detail?

All my birds are in their cages,
Every rose is in a pot;
I get dreamier by stages—
Maybe so—so what?

If you even brush my hand,
Absent-mindedly as this;
Just your touch upon my hand
I can dream into a kiss;
Then the kiss begins to soar
Into love forevermore—
And though your little boat has no anchor,
And my little boat has no sail,
How can a dreamer on love's blue ocean
Be bothered by a slight detail?

All my birds are in their cages,
Every rose is in a pot;
I get dreamier by stages—
Maybe so—so what?

BOB MERRILL

When I Am Not with You

When I am not with you
I am alone,
For there is no one else
And there is nothing
That comforts me but you.
When you are gone
Suddenly I am sick,
Blackness is round me,
There is nothing left.

97

I have tried many things,
Music and cities,
Stars in their constellations
And the sea,
But there is nothing
That comforts me but you;
And my poor pride bows down
Like grass in a rain storm
Drenched with my longing.
The night is unbearable,
Oh, let me go to you
For there is no one,
There is nothing
To comfort me but you.

SARA TEASDALE

If Thou Must Love Me, Let It Be for Naught

If thou must love me, let it be for naught
Except for love's sake only. Do not say,
"I love her for her smile—her look—her way
Of speaking gently,—for a trick of thought
That falls in well with mine, and certes * brought
A sense of pleasant ease on such a day"—
For these things in themselves, Belovèd, may
Be changed, or changed for thee—and love, so wrought,
May be unwrought so. Neither love me for
Thine own dear pity's wiping my cheeks dry:
A creature might forget to weep, who bore
Thy comfort long, and lose thy love thereby!
But love me for love's sake, that evermore
Thou mayst love on, through love's eternity.

ELIZABETH BARRETT BROWNING

---

* certes: certainly

98

Young Love

Within my bed, the whole night thru,
I turn and turn . . . and think of you;
And wonder, when we met to-day,
If you said what you meant to say.
And what you thought I thought you meant
And were you sorry when I went;
And did you get my meaning when. . . .
And then the whole thing through again!
I only hope that somewhere you
Are sleeping badly too!

THEODOSIA GARRISON

O, Whistle and I'll Come to Ye, My Lad

CHORUS

O, whistle an' I'll come to ye, my lad!
O, whistle an' I'll come to ye, my lad!
Tho' father an' mother an' a' should gae mad,
O, whistle an' I'll come to ye, my lad!

But warily tent * when ye come to court me,
And come nae unless the back-yett * be a-jee; *
Syne * up the back-style, and let naebody see,
And come as ye were na comin to me,
And come as ye were na comin to me!

At kirk, or at market, whene'er ye meet me,
Gang by me as tho' that ye car'd na a flie; *
But steal me a blink * o' your bonnie black e'e,
Yet look as ye were na lookin to me,
Yet look as ye were na lookin to me!

* tent: look   * -yett: gate   * a-jee: ajar
* Syne: Then   * flie: fly   * blink: glance

99

Ay vow and protest that ye care na for me,
And whyles * ye may lightly * my beauty a wee; *
But court na anither tho' jokin ye be,
For fear that she wyle * your fancy frae * me,
For fear that she wyle your fancy frae me!

ROBERT BURNS

Mary Ann

He's bought a bed and a table too,
A big tin dish for making stew,
A large flat-iron to iron his shirt,
And a flannel, and a scrubbing brush to wash away the dirt.
And he's bought a pail and basins three,
A coffee pot, a kettle, and a teapot for the tea,
   And a soap-bowl and a ladle,
   And a gridiron and a cradle,
And he's going to marry Mary Ann, that's me!
He's going to marry Mary Ann!

JOSEPH TABRAR

Pierrot

Pierrot stands in the garden
   Beneath a waning moon,
And on his lute he fashions
   A fragile silver tune.

Pierrot plays in the garden,
   He thinks he plays for me,
But I am quite forgotten
   Under the cherry tree.

* whyles: sometimes   * lightly: disparage
* wee: little   * wyle: entice
* frae: from

100

Pierrot plays in the garden,
And all the roses know
That Pierrot loves his music,—
But I love Pierrot.

SARA TEASDALE

Men

They hail you as their morning star
Because you are the way you are.
If you return the sentiment,
They'll try to make you different;
And once they have you, safe and sound,
They want to change you all around.
Your moods and ways they put a curse on;
They'd make of you another person.
They cannot let you go your gait;
They influence and educate.
They'd alter all that they admired.
They make me sick, they make me tired.

DOROTHY PARKER

The River-Merchant's Wife: A Letter

While my hair was still cut straight across my forehead
I played about the front gate, pulling flowers.
You came by on bamboo stilts, playing horse,
You walked about my seat, playing with blue plums.
And we went on living in the village of Chokan:
Two small people, without dislike or suspicion.

At fourteen I married My Lord you.
I never laughed, being bashful.

Lowering my head, I looked at the wall.
Called to, a thousand times, I never looked back.

At fifteen I stopped scowling,
I desired my dust to be mingled with yours
Forever and forever and forever.
Why should I climb the look out?

At sixteen you departed,
You went into far Ku-to-yen, by the river of swirling eddies,
And you have been gone five months.
The monkeys make sorrowful noise overhead.
You dragged your feet when you went out.
By the gate now, the moss is grown, the different mosses,
Too deep to clear them away!
The leaves fall early this autumn, in wind.
The paired butterflies are already yellow with August
Over the grass in the West garden;
They hurt me.   I grow older.
If you are coming down through the narrows of the river Kiang,
Please let me know beforehand,
And I will come out to meet you
                    As far as Cho-fu-Sa.

EZRA POUND
(from the Chinese of Rihaku)

Experience

Some men break your heart in two,
    Some men fawn and flatter,
Some men never look at you;
    And that cleans up the matter.

DOROTHY PARKER

When I Am Dead

When I am dead, my dearest,
    Sing no sad songs for me;
Plant thou no roses at my head,
    Nor shady cypress tree:
Be the green grass above me
    With showers and dewdrops wet:
And if thou wilt, remember,
    And if thou wilt, forget.

I shall not see the shadows,
    I shall not feel the rain;
I shall not hear the nightingale
    Sing on as if in pain:
And dreaming through the twilight
    That doth not rise nor set,
Haply I may remember,
    And haply may forget.

                    CHRISTINA ROSSETTI

Come Night, Come Romeo

Come night; come, Romeo; come, thou day in night;
For thou wilt lie upon the wings of night
Whiter than new snow on a raven's back.—
Come, gentle night,—come, loving, black-brow'd night,
Give me my Romeo; and, when he shall die,
Take him and cut him out in little stars,
And he will make the face of heaven so fine,
That all the world will be in love with night,
And pay no worship to the garish sun.—
O, I have bought the mansion of a love,

But not possest it; and, though I am sold,
Not yet enjoy'd: so tedious is this day,
As is the night before some festival
To an impatient child that hath new robes
And may not wear them.

WILLIAM SHAKESPEARE
(from *Romeo and Juliet*)

Together

A Birthday

My heart is like a singing bird
    Whose nest is in a watered shoot;
My heart is like an apple-tree
    Whose boughs are bent with thick-set fruit;
My heart is like a rainbow shell
    That paddles in a halcyon sea;
My heart is gladder than all these,
    Because my love is come to me.

Raise me a dais of silk and down;
    Hang it with vair and purple dyes;
Carve it in doves and pomegranates,
    And peacocks with a hundred eyes;
Work it in gold and silver grapes,
    In leaves and silver fleurs-de-lys;
Because the birthday of my life
    Is come, my love is come to me.

                CHRISTINA ROSSETTI

Lift your arms to the stars
   And give an immortal shout!
Not all the veils of darkness
   Can put your beauty out.

You are armed with love, with love,
   Nor all the powers of fate
Can touch you with a spear—
   Nor all the hands of hate.

What of good and evil,
   Hell, and Heaven above—
Trample them with love!
   Ride over them with love!

          JOHN HALL WHEELOCK

Recuerdo

We were very tired, we were very merry—
We had gone back and forth all night on the ferry.
It was bare and bright, and smelled like a stable—
But we looked into a fire, we leaned across a table,
We lay on a hill-top underneath the moon;
And the whistles kept blowing, and the dawn came soon.

We were very tired, we were very merry—
We had gone back and forth all night on the ferry;
And you ate an apple, and I ate a pear,
From a dozen of each we had bought somewhere;
And the sky went wan, and the wind came cold,
The sun rose dripping, a bucketful of gold.

We were very tired, we were very merry,
We had gone back and forth all night on the ferry.

We hailed, "Good morrow, mother!" to a shawl-covered head,
And bought a morning paper, which neither of us read;
And she wept, "God bless you!" for the apples and pears,
And we gave her all our money but our subway fares.

EDNA ST. VINCENT MILLAY

Psalm to My Belovèd

Lo, I have opened unto you the wide gates of my being,
And like a tide you have flowed into me.
The innermost recesses of my spirit are full of you, and all the
    channels of my soul are grown sweet with your presence.
For you have brought me peace;
The peace of great tranquil waters, and the quiet of the summer
    sea.
Your hands are filled with peace as the noon-tide is filled with
    light; about your head is bound the eternal quiet of the
    stars, and in your heart dwells the calm miracle of twilight.
I am utterly content.
In all my spirit is no ripple of unrest,
For I have opened unto you the wide gates of my being
And like a tide you have flowed into me.

EUNICE TIETJENS

A Decade

When you came, you were like red wine and honey,
And the taste of you burnt my mouth with its sweetness.
Now you are like morning bread,
I hardly taste you at all for I know your savor,
But I am completely nourished.

AMY LOWELL

A Pavane for the Nursery

Now touch the air softly,
Step gently. One, two . . .
I'll love you till roses
Are robin's-egg blue;
I'll love you till gravel
Is eaten for bread,
And lemons are orange,
And lavender's red.

Now touch the air softly,
Swing gently the broom.
I'll love you till windows
Are all of a room;
And the table is laid,
And the table is bare,
And the ceiling reposes
On bottomless air.

I'll love you till Heaven
Rips the stars from his coat,
And the Moon rows away in
A glass-bottomed boat;
And Orion steps down
Like a diver below,
And Earth is ablaze,
And Ocean aglow.

So touch the air softly,
And swing the broom high.
We will dust the gray mountains,
And sweep the blue sky;
And I'll love you as long
As the furrow the plow,
As However is Ever,
And Ever is Now.

WILLIAM JAY SMITH

Night Ride

Along the black
leather strap
of the night
deserted road

swiftly rolls
the freighted bus.
Huddled together
two lovers doze

their hands linkt
across their laps
their bodies loosely
interlockt

their heads resting
two heavy fruits
on the plaited
basket of their limbs.

Slowly the bus
slides into light.
Here are hills
detach'd from dark

the road uncoils
a white ribbon
the lovers with
the hills unfold

wake cold
to face the fate
of those who love
despite the world.

HERBERT READ

O Mistress Mine

O mistress mine, where are you roaming?
O stay and hear; your true love's coming,
That can sing both high and low.
Trip no further, pretty sweeting;
Journeys end in lovers' meeting,
Every wise man's son doth know.

What is love? 'Tis not hereafter;
Present mirth hath present laughter;
What's to come is still unsure.
In delay there lies no plenty;
Then come kiss me, sweet and twenty;
Youth's a stuff will not endure.

WILLIAM SHAKESPEARE

Lines

to a movement in Mozart's E-flat symphony

Show me again the time
When in the Junetide's prime
We flew by meads and mountains northerly!—
Yea, to such freshness, fairness, fulness, fineness, freeness,
Love lures life on.

Show me again the day
When from the sandy bay
We looked together upon the pestered sea!—
Yea, to such surging, swaying, sighing, swelling, shrinking,
Love lures life on.

Show me again the hour
When by the pinnacled tower

We eyed each other and feared futurity!—
Yea, to such bodings, broodings, beatings, blanchings, blessings,
    Love lures life on.

Show me again just this:
The moment of that kiss
Away from the prancing folk, by the strawberry-tree!—
Yet, to such rashness, ratheness, * rareness, ripeness, richness,
    Love lures life on.

THOMAS HARDY

Love Is Enough

Love is enough: though the World be a-waning
And the woods have no voice but the voice of complaining,
Though the sky be too dark for dim eyes to discover
The gold-cups and daisies fair blooming thereunder,
Though the hills be held shadows, and the sea a dark wonder
And this day draw a veil over all deeds passed over,
Yet their hands shall not tremble, their feet shall not falter;
The void shall not weary, the fear shall not alter
These lips and these eyes of the loved and the lover.

WILLIAM MORRIS

In the dark pine-wood
I would we lay,
In deep cool shadow
At noon of day.

How sweet to lie there,
Sweet to kiss,
Where the great pine-forest
Enaisled is!

---

* ratheness: blooming early in the season

Thy kiss descending
Sweeter were
With a soft tumult
Of thy hair.

O, unto the pine-wood
At noon of day
Come with me now,
Sweet love, away.

JAMES JOYCE

I will make you brooches and toys for your delight
Of bird-song at morning and star-shine at night.
I will make a palace fit for you and me
Of green days in forests and blue days at sea.

I will make my kitchen, and you shall keep your room,
Where white flows the river and bright blows the broom,
And you shall wash your linen and keep your body white
In rainfall at morning and dewfall at night.

And this shall be for music when no one else is near,
The fine song for singing, the rare song to hear!
That only I remember, that only you admire,
Of the broad road that stretches and the roadside fire.

ROBERT LOUIS STEVENSON

The Night of the Full Moon

O come with me into this moonlight world.
The trees are large and soft tonight,
With blossoms loaded soft and white,
A cloud of whiteness furling and unfurled.

The houses give their sounds upon the air
  In muted tones and secrecies,
  Their lights like laughter through the trees.
The evening breathes its vows into our hair.

The evening puts its lips to throat and brow
  And swears what it has sworn before
  To others and will swear to more.
The evening has its arms about us now.

LLOYD FRANKENBERG

Love Comes Quietly

Love comes quietly,
finally, drops
about me, on me,
in the old ways.

What did I know
thinking myself
able to go
alone all the way.

ROBERT CREELEY

Meeting at Night

The grey sea and the long black land;
And the yellow half-moon large and low;
And the startled little waves that leap
In fiery ringlets from their sleep,
As I gain the cove with pushing prow,
And quench its speed in the slushy sand.

Then a mile of warm sea-scented beach;
Three fields to cross till a farm appears;
A tap at the pane, the quick sharp scratch
And blue spurt of a lighted match,
And a voice less loud, through its joys and fears,
Than the two hearts beating each to each!

ROBERT BROWNING

Poet to His Love

An old silver church in a forest
Is my love for you.
The trees around it
Are words that I have stolen from your heart.
An old silver bell, the last smile you gave,
Hangs at the top of my church.
It rings only when you come through the forest
And stand beside it.
And then, it has no need for ringing,
For your voice takes its place.

MAXWELL BODENHEIM

Dear Dark Head

Put your head, darling, darling, darling,
  Your darling black head my heart above;
Oh, mouth of honey, with the thyme for fragrance,
  Who with heart in breast could deny you love?

Oh, many and many a young girl for me is pining,
  Letting her locks of gold to the cold wind free,
For me, the foremost of our gay young fellows;
  But I'd leave a hundred, pure love, for thee!

Then put your head, darling, darling, darling,
  Your darling black head my heart above;
Oh, mouth of honey, with the thyme for fragrance,
  Who, with heart in breast, could deny you love?

SAMUEL FERGUSON

Summmum Bonum

All the breath and the bloom of the year in the bag of one bee:
  All the wonder and wealth of the mine in the heart of one
      gem:
In the core of one pearl all the shade and the shine of the sea:
  Breath and bloom, shade and shine, wonder, wealth, and how
      far above them—
    Truth, that's brighter than gem,
    Trust, that's purer than pearl,—
Brightest truth, purest trust in the universe—
    In the kiss of one girl.

ROBERT BROWNING

Sonnet XXIX

When, in disgrace with fortune and men's eyes,
I all alone beweep my outcast state,
And trouble deaf heaven with my bootless cries,
And look upon myself, and curse my fate,
Wishing me like to one more rich in hope,
Featured like him, like him with friends possess'd,
Desiring this man's art and that man's scope,
With what I most enjoy contented least;
Yet in these thoughts myself almost despising,
Haply I think on thee, and then my state,

117

Like to the lark at break of day arising
From sullen earth, sings hymns at heaven's gate;
  For thy sweet love remember'd such wealth brings
  That then I scorn to change my state with kings.

WILLIAM SHAKESPEARE

Embraceable You

(from the musical "Girl Crazy")

Danny

Dozens of girls would storm up;
  I had to lock my door.
Somehow I couldn't warm up
  To one before.
What was it that controlled me?
  What kept my love-life lean?
My intuition told me
  You'd come on the scene.
Lady, listen to the rhythm of my heart beat,
  And you'll get just what I mean.

Refrain

  Embrace me,
My sweet embraceable you.
  Embrace me,
You irreplaceable you.
Just one look at you—my heart grew tipsy in me;
You and you alone bring out the gypsy in me.
  I love all
The many charms about you;
  Above all
I want my arms about you.
Don't be a naughty baby,
Come to papa—come to papa—do!
My sweet embraceable you.

Molly

I went about reciting,
   "Here's one who'll never fall!"
But I'm afraid the writing
   Is on the wall.
My nose I used to turn up
   When you'd besiege my heart;
Now I completely burn up
   When you're slow to start.
I'm afraid you'll have to take the consequences;
   You upset the apple cart.

Refrain

    Embrace me,
My sweet embraceable you.
    Embrace me,
You irreplaceable you.
In your arms I find love so delectable, dear,
I'm afraid it isn't quite respectable, dear.
    But hang it—
Come on, let's glorify love!
    Ding dang it!
You'll shout "Encore!" if I love.
Don't be a naughty papa,
Come to baby—come to baby—do!
My sweet embraceable you.

IRA GERSHWIN

Kissin'

Some say kissin's ae sin,
   But I say, not at a';
For it's been in the warld
   Ever sin' there were twa.

If it werena lawfu',
   Lawyers wadna' 'low it;
If it werena holy,
   Meenisters wadna' dae it;

If it werena modest,
   Maidens wadna' taste it;
If it werena plenty,
   Poor folk couldna' hae it.

ANONYMOUS

A Leap-Year Episode

Can I forget that winter night
   In eighteen eighty-four,
When Nellie, charming little sprite,
   Came tapping at the door?
"Good evening, miss," I blushing said,
   For in my heart I knew—
And, knowing, hung my pretty head—
   That Nellie came to woo.

She clasped my big, red hand, and fell
   Adown upon her knees,
And cried: "You know I love you well,
   So be my husband, please!"
And then she swore she'd ever be
   A tender wife and true—
Ah, what delight it was to me
   That Nellie came to woo!

She'd lace my shoes and darn my hose
   And mend my shirts, she said;
And grease my comely Roman nose

Each night on going to bed;
She'd build the fires and fetch the coal,
And split the kindling, too—
Love's perjuries o'erwhelmed her soul
When Nellie came to woo.

And as I, blushing, gave no check
To her advances rash,
She twined her arms about my neck,
And toyed with my moustache;
And then she pleaded for a kiss,
While I—what could I do
But coyly yield me to that bliss
When Nellie came to woo?

I am engaged, and proudly wear
A gorgeous diamond ring,
And I shall wed my lover fair
Some time in gentle spring.
I face my doom without a sigh—
And so, forsooth, would you,
If you but loved as fond as I
The Nellie who came to woo.

Attributed to EUGENE FIELD

In a Boat

See the stars, love,
In the water much clearer and brighter
Than those above us, and whiter,
Like nenuphars! *

Star-shadows shine, love:
How many stars in your bowl?

* nenuphars: water lilies

How many shadows in your soul?
Only mine, love, mine?

When I move the oars, see
How the stars are tossed,
Distorted, even lost!
Even yours, do you see?

The poor waters spill
The stars, waters troubled, forsaken!—
The heavens are not shaken, you say, love;
Its stars stand still.

There! did you see
That spark fly up at us? even
Stars are not safe in heaven!
What of me then, love, me?

What then, love, if soon
Your star be tossed over a wave?
Would the darkness look like a grave?
Would you swoon, love, swoon?

D. H. LAWRENCE

Valentine

Chipmunks jump, and
Greensnakes slither.
Rather burst than
Not be with her.

Bluebirds fight, but
Bears are stronger.
We've got fifty
Years or longer.

Hoptoads hop, but
Hogs are fatter.
Nothing else but
us can matter.

DONALD HALL

The Corner of the Field

Here the young lover, on his elbow raised,
Looked at his happy girl with grass surrounded,
And flicked the spotted beetle from her wrist:
She, with head thrown back, at heaven gazed,
At Suffolk clouds, serene and slow and mounded;
Then calmly smiled at him before they kissed.

FRANCES CORNFORD

Love Lost and Love Dead

from *Improvisations: Light and Snow*

IX

This girl gave her heart to me,
And this, and this.
This one looked at me as if she loved me,
And silently walked away.
This one I saw once and loved, and saw her never again.

Shall I count them for you upon my fingers?
Or like a priest solemnly sliding beads?
Or pretend they are roses, pale pink, yellow, and white,
And arrange them for you in a wide bowl
To be set in sunlight?
See how nicely it sounds as I count them for you—
"This girl gave her heart to me
And this, and this". . . !
And nevertheless my heart breaks when I think of them,
When I think their names,
And how, like leaves, they have changed and blown
And will lie at last, forgotten,
Under the snow.

CONRAD AIKEN

Donall Oge:* Grief of a Girl's Heart

It is late last night the dog was speaking of you,
The snipe was speaking of you in her deep marsh,
It is you are the lonely bird throughout the woods,
And that you may be without a mate until you find me.

You promised me and you said a lie to me,
That you would be before me where the sheep are flocked.
I gave a whistle and three hundred cries to you,
And I found nothing there but a bleating lamb.

You promised me a thing that was hard for you,
A ship of gold under a silver mast,
Twelve towns and a market in all of them,
And a fine white court by the side of the sea.

You promised me a thing that is not possible,
That you would give me gloves of the skin of a fish,
That you would give me shoes of the skin of a bird,
And a suit of the dearest silk in Ireland.

My mother said to me not to be talking with you,
To-day or to-morrow or on the Sunday.
It was a bad time she took for telling me that,
It was shutting the door after the house was robbed.

You have taken the east from me, you have taken the west from
　　me,
You have taken what is before me and what is behind me;
You have taken the moon, you have taken the sun from me,
And my fear is great that you have taken God from me.

LADY AUGUSTA GREGORY
(Translated from the Irish)

---

* Donall Oge: young Donald

128

For Anne

With Annie gone,
whose eyes to compare
With the morning sun?

Not that I did compare,
But I do compare
Now that she's gone.

LEONARD COHEN

Sea Love

Tide be runnin' the great world over:
    'Twas only last June month I mind that we
Was thinkin' the toss and the call in the breast of the lover
    So everlastin' as the sea.

Here's the same little fishes that sputter and swim,
    Wi' the moon's old glim on the gray, wet sand;
An' him no more to me nor me to him
    Than the wind goin' over my hand.

CHARLOTTE MEW

Since there's no help, come, let us kiss and part,
Nay, I have done: you get no more of me,
And I am glad, yea glad with all my heart,
That thus so cleanly, I myself can free.
Shake hands for ever, cancel all our vows,
And, when we meet at any time again,
Be it not seen in either of our brows

That we one jot of former love retain.
Now at the last gasp of Love's latest breath,
When, his pulse failing, passion speechless lies,
When Faith is kneeling by his bed of death,
And Innocence is closing up his eyes,
    Now if thou wouldst, when all have given him over,
    From death to life, thou might'st him yet recover.

MICHAEL DRAYTON

Annabel Lee

It was many and many a year ago,
    In a kingdom by the sea,
That a maiden there lived whom you may know
    By the name of Annabel Lee;
And this maiden she lived with no other thought
    Than to love and be loved by me.

I was a child and she was a child,
    In this kingdom by the sea:
But we loved with a love that was more than love—
    I and my Annabel Lee;
With a love that the winged seraphs of heaven
    Coveted her and me.

And this was the reason that, long ago,
    In this kingdom by the sea,
A wind blew out of a cloud, chilling
    My beautiful Annabel Lee;
So that her highborn kinsman came
    And bore her away from me,
To shut her up in a sepulchre
    In this kingdom by the sea.

The angels, not half so happy in heaven,
  Went envying her and me—
Yes!—that was the reason (as all men know,
  In this kingdom by the sea)
That the wind came out of the cloud by night,
  Chilling and killing my Annabel Lee.

But our love it was stronger by far than the love
  Of those who were older than we—
  Of many far wiser than we—
And neither the angels in heaven above,
  Nor the demons down under the sea,
Can ever dissever my soul from the soul
  Of the beautiful Annabel Lee:—

For the moon never beams, without bringing me dreams
  Of the beautiful Annabel Lee;
And the stars never rise but I see the bright eyes
  Of the beautiful Annabel Lee;
And so, all the night-tide, I lie down by the side
Of my darling, my darling, my life and my bride,
  In her sepulchre there by the sea—
  In her tomb by the sounding sea.

EDGAR ALLAN POE

Non Sum Qualis Eram Bonae Sub Regno Cynarae

Last night, ah, yesternight, betwixt her lips and mine
There fell thy shadow, Cynara! thy breath was shed
Upon my soul between the kisses and the wine;
And I was desolate and sick of an old passion,
  Yea, I was desolate and bowed my head:
I have been faithful to thee, Cynara! in my fashion.

All night upon mine heart I felt her warm heart beat,
Night-long within mine arms in love and sleep she lay;
Surely the kisses of her bought red mouth were sweet;
But I was desolate and sick of an old passion,
    When I awoke and found the dawn was gray:
I have been faithful to thee, Cynara! in my fashion.

I have forgot much, Cynara! gone with the wind,
Flung roses, roses riotously with the throng,
Dancing, to put thy pale, lost lilies out of mind;
But I was desolate and sick of an old passion,
    Yea, all the time, because the dance was long:
I have been faithful to thee, Cynara! in my fashion.

I cried for madder music and for stronger wine,
But when the feast is finished and the lamps expire,
Then falls thy shadow, Cynara! the night is thine;
And I am desolate and sick of an old passion,
    Yea, hungry for the lips of my desire:
I have been faithful to thee, Cynara! in my fashion.

ERNEST DOWSON

There's Wisdom in Women

"Oh love is fair, and love is rare"; my dear one she said,
"But love goes lightly over." I bowed her foolish head,
And kissed her hair and laughed at her. Such a child was she;
So new to love, so true to love, and she spoke so bitterly.

But there's wisdom in women, of more than they have known,
And thoughts go blowing through them, are wiser than their
    own,
Or how should my dear one, being ignorant and young,
Have cried on love so bitterly, with so true a tongue?

RUPERT BROOKE

Were You on the Mountain?

O, were you on the mountain, or saw you my love?
Or saw you my own one, my queen and my dove?
Or saw you the maiden with the step firm and free?
And say, is she pining in sorrow like me?

I was upon the mountain, and saw there your love,
I saw there your own one, your queen and your dove;
I saw there the maiden with the step firm and free,
And she was *not* pining in sorrow like thee.

DOUGLAS HYDE
(Translated from the Irish)

Sigh No More

Sigh no more, ladies, sigh no moe,
  Men were deceivers ever;
One foot in sea, and one on shore,
  To one thing constant never.
    Then sigh not so,
    But let them go,
  And be you blithe and bonny,
Converting all your sighs of woe
  Into Hey nonny, nonny.

Sing no more ditties, sing no moe
  Of dumps so dull and heavy;
The fraud of men was ever so,
  Since summer first was leavy.
    Then sigh not so,
    But let them go,
  And be you blithe and bonny,
Converting all your sighs of woe
  Into Hey nonny, nonny.

WILLIAM SHAKESPEARE

To . . .

When I loved you, I can't but allow
    I had many an exquisite minute;
But the scorn that I feel for you now
    Hath even more luxury in it!

Thus, whether we're on or we're off,
    Some witchery seems to await you;
To love you is pleasant enough,
    But oh! 'tis delicious to hate you!

THOMAS MOORE

The Despairing Lover

Distracted with care,
For Phillis the fair;
Since nothing could move her,
Poor Damon, her lover,
Resolves in despair
No longer to languish,
But, mad with his love,
To precipice goes;
Where, a leap from above
Would soon finish his woes.

    When in rage he came there,
Beholding how steep
The sides did appear,
And the bottom how deep;
His torments projecting,
And sadly reflecting,
That a lover forsaken
A new love may get;
But a neck, when once broken,

Can never be set:
And, that he could die
Whenever he would;
But, that he could live
But as long as he could:

How grievous soever
The torment might grow,
He scorned to endeavour
To finish it so.
But bold, unconcern'd
At thoughts of the pain,
He calmly returned
To his cottage again.

WILLIAM WALSH

She Walked Unaware

Oh, she walked unaware of her own increasing beauty
That was holding men's thoughts from market or plough,
As she passed by intent on her womanly duties
And she passed without leisure to be wayward or proud;
Or if she had pride then it was not in her thinking
But thoughtless in her body like a flower of good breeding.
The first time I saw her spreading coloured linen
Beyond the green willow she gave me gentle greeting
With no more intention than the leaning willow tree.

Though she smiled without intention yet from that day forward
Her beauty filled like water the four corners of my being,
And she rested in my heart like a hare in the form
That is shaped to herself. And I that would be singing
Or whistling at all times went silently then,
Till I drew her aside among straight stems of beeches
When the blackbird was sleeping and she promised that never

The fields would be riped but I'd gather all sweetness,
A red moon of August would rise on our wedding.

October is spreading bright flame along stripped willows,
Low fires of the dogwood burn down to grey water,—
God pity me now and all desolate sinners
Demented with beauty! I have blackened my thought
In drouths of bad longing, and all brightness goes shrouded
Since he came with his rapture of wild words that mirrored
Her beauty and made her ungentle and proud.
To-night she will spread her brown hair on his pillow,
But I shall be hearing the harsh cries of wild fowl.

PATRICK MACDONOGH

Why So Pale and Wan

Why so pale and wan, fond lover?
   Prithee why so pale?
Will, when looking well can't move her,
   Looking ill prevail?
   Prithee why so pale?

Why so dull and mute, young sinner?
   Prithee why so mute?
Will, when speaking well can't win her,
   Saying nothing do't?
   Prithee why so mute?

Quit, quit for shame; this will not move,
   This cannot take her;
If of herself she will not love,
   Nothing can make her:
   The devil take her!

SIR JOHN SUCKLING

Parting after a Quarrel

You looked at me with eyes grown bright with pain,
    Like some trapped thing's. And then you moved your head
Slowly from side to side, as though the strain
    Ached in your throat with anger and with dread.

And then you turned and left me, and I stood
    With a queer sense of deadness over me,
And only wondered dully that you could
    Fasten your trench-coat up so carefully—

Till you were gone. Then all the air was quick
    With my last words, that seemed to leap and quiver;
And in my heart I heard the little click
    Of a door that closes—quietly, forever.

EUNICE TIETJENS

An Expostulation

When late I attempted your pity to move,
    What made you so deaf to my prayers?
Perhaps it was right to dissemble your love,
    But—why did you kick me down stairs?

ISAAC BICKERSTAFF

Never Seek to Tell Thy Love

Never seek to tell thy love,
Love that never told can be;
For the gentle wind does move
Silently, invisibly.

I told my love, I told my love,
I told her all my heart;
Trembling, cold, in ghastly fears,
Ah! she doth depart.

Soon as she was gone from me,
A traveler came by,
Silently, invisibly:
He took her with a sigh.

WILLIAM BLAKE

False! or Inconstancy

False though she be to me and love,
    I'll ne'er pursue revenge;
For still the charmer I approve,
    Though I deplore her change.

In hours of bliss we oft have met,
    They could not always last;
And though the present I regret,
    I'm grateful for the past.

WILLIAM CONGREVE

 ## The Walk on the Beach

The evening, blue, voluptuous, of June
Settled slowly on the beach with pulsating wings,
Like a sea-gull come to rest: far, far off twinkled
Gold lights from the towers of a city and a passing ship.
The dark sea rolled its body at the end of the beach,
The warm soft beach which it was too tired to climb,

And we two walked together there
Arm in arm, having nothing in our souls but love.

Your face shaded by the hat looked up at me;
Your pale face framed in the dark gold of your hair,
A look I have only once seen, that I shall never see again.
Our steps were lost on the long vast carpet of sand,
Our souls were lost in the sky where the stars came out;
Our bodies clung together: time was not.
Love came and passed: our lives were cleaned and changed.

The winter will spill upon us soon its dark cruse * laden with
    rain,
Time has broken our moorings; we have drifted apart; love is
    done.
I can only dream in the long still nights that we rest heart to
    heart,
I can only wake to the knowledge that my love is lost and won.
We were as two weak swallows, together to southward set,
Blown apart, vainly crying to each other while at strife with the
    seas.
We go out in the darkness; we speak but in memories;
But I have never forgotten and I shall never forget.

JOHN GOULD FLETCHER

Your Little Hands

Your little hands,
Your little feet,
Your little mouth—
Oh, God, how sweet!

Your little nose,
Your little ears,

* cruse: an earthen pot

139

Your eyes, that shed
Such little tears!

Your little voice,
So soft and kind;
Your little soul,
Your little mind!

SAMUEL HOFFENSTEIN

Down By the Salley Gardens

Down by the salley gardens my love and I did meet;
She passed the salley gardens with little snow-white feet.
She bid me take love easy, as the leaves grow on the tree;
But, I being young and foolish, with her would not agree.
In a field by the river my love and I did stand,
And on my leaning shoulder she laid her snow-white hand.
She bid me take life easy, as the grass grows on the weirs;
But I was young and foolish, and now am full of tears.

W. B. YEATS

A Tune

A foolish rhythm turns in my idle head
As a wind-mill turns in the wind on an empty sky.
Why it is when love, which men call deathless, is dead,
That memory, men call fugitive, will not die?
Is love not dead? yet I hear that tune if I lie
Dreaming awake in the night on my lonely bed,
And an old thought turns with the old tune in my head
As a wind-mill turns in the wind on an empty sky.

ARTHUR SYMONS

The Banks O' Doon

Ye banks and braes * o' bonnie Doon,
  How can ye bloom sae fresh and fair?
How can ye chant, ye little birds,
  And I sae weary fu' o' care!
Thou'll break my heart, thou warbling bird,
  That wantons thro' the flowering thorn!
Thou minds me o' departed joys,
  Departed never to return.

Aft hae I rov'd by bonnie Doon
  To see the rose and woodbine twine,
And ilka * bird sang o' its luve,
  And fondly sae did I o' mine.
Wi' lightsome heart I pu'd * a rose,
  Fu' sweet upon its thorny tree!
And my fause luver staw * my rose—
  But ah! he left the thorn wi' me.

ROBERT BURNS

The Spring and the Fall

In the spring of the year, in the spring of the year,
I walked the road beside my dear.
The trees were black where the bark was wet.
I see them yet, in the spring of the year.
He broke me a bough of the blossoming peach
That was out of the way and hard to reach.

In the fall of the year, in the fall of the year,
I walked the road beside my dear.
The rooks went up with a raucous trill.

* braes: slopes   * ilka: every   * pu'd: plucked
* fause luver staw: false lover stole

141

I hear them still, in the fall of the year.
He laughed at all I dared to praise,
And broke my heart, in little ways.

Year be springing or year be falling,
The bark will drip and the birds be calling.
There's much that's fine to see and hear
In the spring of a year, in the fall of a year.
'Tis not love's going hurts my days,
But that it went in little ways.

EDNA ST. VINCENT MILLAY

Winter

- The tree still bends over the lake,
- And I try to recall our love,
- Our love which had a thousand leaves.

SHEILA WINGFIELD

Patterns

I walk down the garden-paths,
And all the daffodils
Are blowing, and the bright blue squills.
I walk down the patterned garden-paths
In my stiff, brocaded gown.
With my powdered hair and jewelled fan,
I too am a rare
Pattern. As I wander down
The garden-paths.

My dress is richly figured,
And the train

Makes a pink and silver stain
On the gravel, and the thrift
Of the borders.
Just a plate of current fashion,
Tripping by in high-heeled, ribboned shoes.
Not a softness anywhere about me,
Only whale-bone and brocade.
And I sink on a seat in the shade
Of a lime-tree. For my passion
Wars against the stiff brocade.
The daffodils and squills
Flutter in the breeze
As they please.
And I weep;
For the lime-tree is in blossom
And one small flower has dropped upon my bosom.

And the splashing of waterdrops
In the marble fountain
Comes down the garden-paths.
The dripping never stops.
Underneath my stiffened gown
Is the softness of a woman bathing in a marble basin,
A basin in the midst of hedges grown
So thick, she cannot see her lover hiding.
She guesses he is near,
And the sliding of the water
Seems the stroking of a dear
Hand upon her.
What is Summer in a fine brocaded gown!
I should like to see it lying in a heap upon the ground.
All the pink and silver crumpled upon the ground.

I would be the pink and silver as I ran along the paths,
And he would stumble after,
Bewildered by my laughter.

I should see the sun flashing from his sword-hilt and the buckles
    on his shoes.
I would choose
To lead him in a maze along the patterned paths,
A bright and laughing maze for my heavy-booted lover,
Till he caught me in the shade,
And the buttons of his waistcoat bruised my body as he clasped
    me,
Aching, melting, unafraid.
With the shadows of the leaves and the sundrops,
And the plopping of the waterdrops,
All about us in the open afternoon—
I am very like to swoon
With the weight of this brocade.
For the sun sifts through the shade.

Underneath the fallen blossom
In my bosom,
Is a letter I have hid.
It was brought to me this morning by a rider from the Duke.
"Madam, we regret to inform you that Lord Hartwell
Died in action Thursday se'nnight."
As I read it in the white, morning sunlight,
The letters squirmed like snakes.
"Any answer, Madam?" said my footman.
"No," I told him.
"See that the messenger takes some refreshment.
No, no answer."
And I walked into the garden,
Up and down the patterned paths,
In my stiff, correct brocade.
The blue and yellow flowers stood up proudly in the sun,
Each one.
I stood upright too,
Held rigid to the pattern
By the stiffness of my gown.

Up and down I walked,
Up and down.

In a month he would have been my husband.
In a month, here, underneath this lime,
We would have broke the pattern;
He for me, and I for him,
He as Colonel, I as Lady,
On this shady seat.
He had a whim
That sunlight carried blessing.
And I answered, "It shall be as you have said."
Now he is dead.

In Summer and in Winter I shall walk
Up and down
The patterned garden-paths
In my stiff, brocaded gown.
The squills and daffodils
Will give place to pillared roses, and to asters, and to snow.
I shall go
Up and down,
In my gown.
Gorgeously arrayed,
Boned and stayed.
And the softness of my body will be guarded from embrace
By each button, hook, and lace.
For the man who should loose me is dead,
Fighting with the Duke in Flanders,
In a pattern called a war.
Christ! What are patterns for?

AMY LOWELL

Love Stories

Love Stories

The Kiss

Give me, my love, that billing kiss
   I taught you one delicious night,
When, turning epicures in bliss,
   We tried inventions of delight.

Come, gently steal my lips along
   And let your lips in murmurs move,—
Ah, no!—again—that kiss was wrong—
   How can you be so dull, my love?

"Cease, cease!" the blushing girl replied—
   And in her milky arms she caught me—
"How can you thus your pupil chide;
   You know *'twas in the dark* you taught me!"

THOMAS MOORE

Pretty Polly

"Pretty Polly goes dressed in red;
Her laughing lips have bestown no favor
But I'd stand all day on the top of my head
For a taste of their hurtsome flavor.

"A true-love never goes gay, goes gay,
A scarlet dress is the badge of folly;
The gown of a true-love's drab, some say,
But red suits pretty Polly.

"When pretty Polly is seen abroad
Be sure there's always a beau to squire her
Around the stones in the rocky road
And lift her over the mire.

"For he cares not for his Sunday suit
By half so much as a miser's measure,
Nor takes a thought if he scuffs his boot
For pretty Polly's pleasure.

"Son, the counsel I give to you
Is, shun the lass in a skirt of folly.
But who'd give a hang for a lover that's true
If he could win pretty Polly?

"What lad has eyes for their hodden gray *
Or a glance to spare for the dowdy lasses
Or half an ear for a word they say
When, laughing, Polly passes?

"I courted Polly in shade and shine,
Her hands met mine with their touch of fire
But she would not set me a table to dine
On the food of my heart's desire.

---

* hodden gray: coarse homemade cloth

"The girl I took to my board and bed
Is kind of heart, and she's plump and jolly;
She has caused me no grief since ever we wed,
But she is not pretty Polly.

"And pretty Polly will never be mine,—
To love her still is the height of folly
But as long as the sun has the strength to shine
I'll long for pretty Polly.

"I'll long for pretty Polly."

BYRON HERBERT REECE

After Ever Happily

or

The Princess and the Woodcutter

And they both lived happily ever after . . .
The wedding was held in the palace. Laughter
Rang to the roof as a loosened rafter
Crashed down and squashed the chamberlain flat—
And how the wedding guests chuckled at that!
"You, with your horny indelicate hands,
Who drop your haitches and call them 'ands,
Who cannot afford to buy her a dress,
How dare you presume to pinch our princess—
Miserable woodcutter, uncombed, unwashed!"
Were the chamberlain's words (before he was squashed).
"Take her," said the Queen, who had a soft spot
For woodcutters. "He's strong and he's handsome. Why not?"
"What rot!" said the King, but he dare not object;
The Queen wore the trousers—that's as you'd expect.
Said the chamberlain, usually meek and inscrutable,

"A princess and a woodcutter? The match is unsuitable."
Her dog barked its welcome again and again.
It was roaring with pain—I mean pouring with rain,
As they came to the palace. "Go in, sweet love,"
Said the P. to the W. and gave him a shove.
And the princess gulped, "You bet your life!"
"Darling," said the woodcutter, "will you be my wife?"
So he nursed her to health with some help from his mother,
And lifted her, horribly hurt, from her tumble.
A woodcutter, watching, saw the horse stumble,
As she rode through the woods, a princess in her prime
On a dapple-gray horse . . . Now, to finish my rhyme,
I'll start it properly: Once upon a time—

IAN SERRAILLIER

A Spinning-Wheel Song

Mellow the moonlight to shine is beginning;
Close by the window young Eileen is spinning;
Bent o'er the fire, her blind grandmother, sitting,
Is croaning, and moaning, and drowsily knitting:
"Eileen, achora, I hear some one tapping."
" 'Tis the ivy, dear mother, against the glass flapping."
"Eileen, I surely hear somebody sighing."
" 'Tis the sound, mother dear, of the summer wind dying."
Merrily, cheerily, noisily whirring,
Swings the wheel, spins the reel, while the foot's stirring;
Sprightly, and lightly, and airily ringing,
Thrills the sweet voice of the young maiden singing.

"What's that noise that I hear at the window, I wonder?"
" 'Tis the little birds chirping the holly-bush under."

152

What makes you be shoving and moving your stool on,
And singing all wrong that old song of 'The Coolun?' "
There's a form at the casement—the form of her true-love;
Get up on the stool, through the lattice step lightly,
We'll rove in the grove while the moon's shining brightly."
Merrily, cheerily, noisily whirring,
Swings the wheel, spins the reel, while the foot's stirring;
Sprightly, and lightly, and airily ringing,
Thrills the sweet voice of the young maiden singing.

The maid shakes her head, on her lip lays her fingers,
Steals up from her seat—longs to go, and yet lingers;
A frighten'd glance turns to her drowsy grandmother,
Puts one foot on the stool, spins the wheel with the other.
Lazily, easily, swings now the wheel round;
Slowly and slowly is heard now the reel's sound;
Noiseless and light to the lattice above her
The maid steps—then leaps to the arms of her lover.
Slower—and slower—and slower the wheel swings;
Lower—and lower—and lower the reel rings;
Ere the reel and the wheel stopp'd their ringing and moving,
Through the grove the young lovers by moonlight are roving.

JOHN FRANCIS WALLER

Oh see how thick the goldcup flowers
    Are lying in field and lane,
With dandelions to tell the hours
    That never are told again.
Oh may I squire you round the meads
    And pick you posies gay?
—'Twill do no harm to take my arm.
    "You may, young man, you may."

Ah, spring was sent for lass and lad,
  'Tis now the blood runs gold,
And man and maid had best be glad
  Before the world is old.
What flowers to-day may flower tomorrow,
  But never as good as new.
—Suppose I wound my arm right round—
  " 'Tis true, young men, 'tis true."

Some lads there are, 'tis shame to say,
  That only court to thieve,
And once they bear the bloom away
  'Tis little enough they leave.
Then keep your heart for men like me
  And safe from trustless chaps.
My love is true and all for you.
  "Perhaps, young man, perhaps."

*　*　*

Oh, look in my eyes, then, can you doubt?
  —Why, 'tis a mile from town.
How green the grass is all about!
  We might as well sit down.
—Ah, life, what is it but a flower?
  Why must true lovers sigh?
Be kind, have pity, my own, my pretty,—
  "Good-bye, young man, good-bye."

                         A. E. HOUSMAN

Moon Door

I know a moon door in the Forbidden City:
in the Emperor Chien-lung's apartment this door is standing.
Through it I have seen pass the ghosts of an old ceremony . . .

Forty-eight serving men bearing the forty-eight dishes that contained the Emperor's dinner.
But the Emperor was in love. He would touch nothing.
He sat staring at the double tree in the garden,
thinking of the fragrant lady
who had come but a season before from the land of Zungaria.
And back through the moon door I have seen them trooping,
bearing the untasted food in forty-eight green and yellow dishes.
Silent they go, leaving him staring at the garden,
leaving him sighing that none would dare a word of comfort or advice.

MARY KENNEDY

The Highwayman

PART ONE

The wind was a torrent of darkness among the gusty trees,
The moon was a ghostly galleon tossed upon cloudy seas,
The road was a ribbon of moonlight over the purple moor,
     And the highwayman came riding,
       Riding, riding,
The highwayman came riding, up to the old inn-door.

He'd a French cocked-hat on his forehead, a bunch of lace at his chin,
A coat of the claret velvet, and breeches of brown doeskin;
They fitted with never a wrinkle; his boots were up to the thigh!
     And he rode with a jeweled twinkle,
       His pistol butts a-twinkle,
His rapier hilt a-twinkle, under the jeweled sky.

Over the cobbles he clattered and clashed in the dark inn-yard,
And he tapped with his whip on the shutters, but all was
    locked and barred;
He whistled a tune to the window, and who should be waiting
    there
        But the landlord's black-eyed daughter,
        Bess, the landlord's daughter,
Plaiting a dark red love knot into her long black hair.

And dark in the dark old inn-yard a stable-wicket creaked
Where Tim the ostler listened; his face was white and peaked;
His eyes were hollows of madness, his hair like moldy hay,
        But he loved the landlord's daughter,
        The landlord's red-lipped daughter,
Dumb as a dog he listened, and he heard the robber say:

"One kiss, my bonny sweetheart, I'm after a prize tonight,
But I shall be back with the yellow gold before the morning
    light;
Yet, if they press me sharply, and harry me through the day,
        Then look for me by moonlight
        Watch for me by moonlight,
I'll come to thee my moonlight, though hell should bar the
    way."

He rose upright in the stirrups; he scarce could reach her hand,
But she loosened her hair i' the casement! His face burnt like
    a brand
As the black cascade of perfume came tumbling over his breast;
        And he kissed its waves in the moonlight,
        (Oh, sweet black waves in the moonlight!)
Then he tugged at his rein in the moonlight, and galloped
    away to the West.

PART TWO

He did not come in the dawning: he did not come at noon;
And out o' the tawny sunset, before the rise o' the moon,

When the road was a gypsy's ribbon, looping the purple moor,
    A red-coat troop came marching,
      Marching, marching,
King George's men came marching, up to the old inn-door.

They said no word to the landlord, they drank his ale instead,
But they gagged his daughter and bound her to the foot of her
    narrow bed;
Two of them knelt at her casement, with muskets at their side!
    There was death at every window;
    And hell at one dark window;
For Bess could see, through her casement, the road that *he*
    would ride.

They had tied her up to attention, with many a sniggering jest;
They had bound a musket beside her, with the barrel beneath
    her breast!
"Now keep good watch!" and they kissed her.
She heard the dead man say—
    Look for me by moonlight;
    Watch for me by moonlight;
I'll come to thee by moonlight, though hell should bar the way!

She twisted her hands behind her; but all the knots held good!
She writhed her hands till her fingers were wet with sweat or
    blood!
They stretched and strained in the darkness, and the hours
    crawled by like years,
    Till, now, on the stroke of midnight,
    Cold, on the stroke of midnight,
The tip of one finger touched it! The trigger at least was hers!

The tip of one finger touched it; she strove no more for the rest!
Up, she stood up to attention, with the barrel beneath her
    breast,
She would not risk their hearing! she would not strive again;
    For the road lay bare in the moonlight,

Blank and bare in the moonlight;
And the blood of her veins in the moonlight throbbed to her
love's refrain.

Tlot-tlot, tlot-tlot! Had they heard it? The horse-hoofs ringing
clear;
Tlot-tlot, tlot-tlot, in the distance? Were they deaf that they did
not hear?
Down the ribbon of moonlight, over the brow of the hill,
The highwayman came riding,
Riding, riding!
The red-coats looked to their priming! She stood up, straight
and still!

Tlot-tlot, in the frosty silence! *Tlot-tlot,* in the echoing night!
Nearer he came and nearer! Her face was like a light!
Her eyes grew wide for a moment! she drew one last deep
breath,
Then her finger moved in the moonlight,
Her musket shattered the moonlight,
Shattered her breast in the moonlight and warned him—with
her death.

He turned; he spurred to the West; he did not know she stood
Bowed, with her head o'er the musket, drenched with her own
red blood!
Not till the dawn he heard it; his face grew gray to hear
How Bess, the landlord's daughter,
The landlord's black-eyed daughter,
Had watched for her love in the moonlight, and died in the
darkness there.

Back, he spurred like a madman, shrieking a curse to the sky,
With the white road smoking behind him and his rapier bran-
dished high!
Blood-red were his spurs i' the golden noon; wine-red was his
velvet coat,

When they shot him down on the highway,
Down like a dog on the highway,
And he lay in his blood on the highway, with the bunch of lace
at his throat.

And still of a winter's night, they say, when the wind is in the
trees,
When the moon is a ghostly galleon tossed upon cloudy seas,
When the road is a ribbon of moonlight over the purple moor,
A highwayman comes riding,
Riding, riding,
A highwayman comes riding, up to the old inn-door.

Over the cobbles he clatters and clangs in the dark inn-yard;
He taps with his whip on the shutters, but all is locked and
barred;
He whistles a tune to the window, and who should be waiting
there
But the landlord's black-eyed daughter,
Bess, the landlord's daughter,
Plaiting a dark red love knot into her long black hair.

ALFRED NOYES

Lily McQueen

(A Ballet, Pas de Deux)

Cool as a cucumber,
Cucumber, cucumber,
In belled, swaying muslin
Waltzed Lily McQueen:

But the eye of Lord Oliver,
(Wicked Lord Oliver)
The eye of Lord Oliver
Burnt grass from the green.

As he caprioled * over
And over and over,
As he caprioled over
The daisies between.

"Find a rhyme for this lady,
This water-clear maidy,
Find a rhyme this lorn lady
To shield from the sun!"

And the eyes of Miss Lily
Dipped daffadowndilly,
While her round lips grew stilly
And shaped to a "Come!"

As she leapt from her lover
With swoon and recover
Lest he should discover
Her secret was one

That was known the world over,
From Cork to Cordova,
That love burns a candle
More fierce than the sun.

So they twined in a tangle
Of love-lyric spangle
As the music's bright jangle
Emblazoned their song

That was older and bolder
Than his look as he told her
That passion's bright smoulder
Beat his heart like a gong!

---

* caprioled: capered, leapt

Oh, such flowery, bowery,
Sunshine and showery
Peace of love's dowry
Will never be seen,

As when Frederick Oliver
(Wicked Lord Oliver)
Caprioled over
To Lily McQueen.

SARA JACKSON

An Original Love-Story

He struggled to kiss her. She struggled the same
  To prevent him so bold and undaunted;
But, as smitten by lightning, he heard her exclaim,
  "Avaunt, Sir!" and off he avaunted.

But when he returned, with the fiendishest laugh,
  Showing clearly that he was affronted,
And threatened by main force to carry her off,
  She cried "Don't" and the poor fellow donted.

When he meekly approached, and sat down at her feet,
  Praying aloud, as before he had ranted,
That she would forgive him and try to be sweet,
  And said "can't you!" the dear girl recanted.

Then softly he whispered, "How could you do so?
  I certainly thought I was jilted;
But come thou with me, to the parson we'll go;
  Say, wilt thou, my dear?" and she wilted.

ANONYMOUS

161

The Juniper Tree

Meet me my love, meet me my love
By the low branching juniper tree
O I will meet you there my love
If no harm come to me
If no harm come to me

Blue burns the cone, blue burns the cone
Of the low branching juniper tree
And there he waited for his love
As the black minutes go by
As the black minutes go by

Bellows in the field a cow, in the field a cow
Bellows loud after its dead calf
As he waited by the juniper tree
And he heard the red fox cough
He heard the red fox cough

Flew through the air, flew through the air an owl
To the low branching juniper tree
As he waited there for his love
And the black minutes went by
And the black minutes went by

The wind blew down, the wind blew down
Into the low branching juniper tree
And all the seeds rattled in the weed
As the wind blew sudden by
As the wind blew sudden by

Then fell the rain, then fell the rain down
Fell cold into black wet sleet
On the low branching juniper tree
And he said why is she late
He said why is she late

I have come to you my love, my love
Waiting by the juniper tree
And he turns to see her standing there
As white as death was she
As white as death was she

Then why are you so long my love, my love
As I waited at the juniper tree?
But now I will kiss your mouth, he said
O never you will, said she
O never you will, said she

WILFRED WATSON

Polly Perkins

I am a broken-hearted, milkman, in grief I'm arrayed,
Through keeping of the company of a young servant maid,
Who lived on board wages to keep the house clean
In a gentleman's family near Paddington Green.

Chorus

She was as beautiful as a butterfly
And as proud as a Queen
Was pretty Polly Perkins of
Paddington Green.

Her eyes were as black as the pips of a pear,
No roses in the garden with her cheeks could compare,
Her hair hung in ringlets so beautiful and long,
I thought that she loved me but I found I was wrong.

When I asked her to marry me she said Oh! what stuff,
And told me to drop it, for she had quite enough
Of my nonsense—at the same time I'd been very kind,
But to marry a milkman she did not feel inclined.

163

Oh, the man that has me must have silver and gold,
A chariot to ride in and be handsome and bold,
His hair must be curly as any watch spring,
And his whiskers as long as a brush for clothing.

In six months she married, this hard-hearted girl,
But it was not a wicount, and it was not a nearl,
It was not a baronite, but a shade or two wuss,
It was a bow-legged conductor of a Twopenny Bus.

ANONYMOUS

Lanty Leary

Bold Lanty was in love, you see, with lively Rosie Carey,
But her father wouldn't give the girl to slippery Lanty Leary;
   Come on for fun, says she, we'll run,
   My father's so contrairy,
Won't you follow me where'er I be? I will, says Lanty Leary.

One day her father died on her, and not from drinking water,
House, land, and cash he left, they say, by will to Rose his
    daughter,
   Come on for fun, says she, we'll run
   To a place more bright and airy,
Won't you follow me where'er I be? More than ever now, says
    Leary.

But Rose herself was taken ill and each day worse was growing,
And Lanty dear, says she, I fear into my grave I'm going;
   You can't survive, says she, nor thrive
   Without your Rosie Carey
Won't you follow me where'er I be? I'll not, says Lanty Leary.

SAMUEL LOVER

The Hill

Breathless, we flung us on the windy hill,
　　Laughed in the sun, and kissed the lovely grass.
　　You said, "Through glory and ecstasy we pass;
Wind, sun, and earth remain, the birds sing still,
When we are old, are old. . . ." "And when we die
　　All's over that is ours; and life burns on
Through other lovers, other lips," said I,
—"Heart of my heart, our heaven is now, is won!"

"We are Earth's best, that learnt her lesson here.
　　Life is our cry. We have kept the faith!" we said;
　　"We shall go down with unreluctant tread
Rose-crowned into the darkness!" . . . Proud we were,
And laughed, that had such brave true things to say.
—And then you suddenly cried, and turned away.

RUPERT BROOKE

The Song of Wandering Aengus

I went out to the hazel wood,
Because a fire was in my head,
And cut and peeled a hazel wand,
And hooked a berry to a thread;
And when white moths were on the wing,
And moth-like stars were flickering out,
I dropped the berry in a stream
And caught a little silver trout.

When I had laid it on the floor
I went to blow the fire aflame,
But something rustled on the floor,

And some one called me by my name:
It had become a glimmering girl
With apple blossom in her hair
Who called me by my name and ran
And faded through the brightening air.

Though I am old with wandering
Through hollow lands and hilly lands,
I will find out where she has gone,
And kiss her lips and take her hands;
And walk among long dappled grass,
And pluck till time and times are done
The silver apples of the moon,
The golden apples of the sun.

W. B. YEATS

Blow Me Eyes!

When I was young and full o' pride,
  A-standin' on the grass
And gazin' o'er the water-side,
  I seen a fisher lass.
"O, fisher lass, be kind awhile,"
  I asks 'er quite unbid.
"Please look into me face and smile"—
  And, blow me eyes, she did!

O, blow me light and blow me blow,
I didn't think she'd charm me so—
  But, blow me eyes, she did!

She seemed so young and beautiful
  I *had* to speak perlite,
(The afternoon was long and dull,

But she was short and bright).
"This ain't no place," I says, "to stand—
  Let's take a walk instid,
Each holdin' of the other's hand"—
  And, blow me eyes, she did!

O, blow me light and blow me blow,
I sort o' thunk she wouldn't go—
  But, blow me eyes, she did!

And as we walked along a lane
  With no one else to see,
Me heart was filled with sudden pain,
  And so I says to she:
"If you would have me actions speak
  The words what can't be hid,
You'd sort o' let me kiss yer cheek"—
  And, blow me eyes, she did!

O, blow me light and blow me blow,
How sweet she was I didn't know—
  But, blow me eyes, *she* did!

But pretty soon me shipmate Jim
  Came strollin' down the beach,
And she began a-oglin' him
  As pretty as a peach.
"O, fickle maid o' false intent,"
  Inpulsively I chid,
"Why don't you go and wed that gent?"
  And, blow me eyes, she did!

O, blow me light and blow me blow,
I didn't think she'd treat me so—
  But, blow me eyes, she did!

WALLACE IRWIN

Aghadoe

There's a glade in Aghadoe, Aghadoe, Aghadoe,
There's a green and silent glade in Aghadoe,
Where we met, my love and I, Love's fair planet in the sky,
O'er that sweet and silent glade in Aghadoe.

There's a glen in Aghadoe, Aghadoe, Aghadoe,
There's a deep and secret glen in Aghadoe,
Where I hid from the eyes of the red-coats and their spies,
That year the trouble came to Aghadoe.

O, my curse on one black heart in Aghadoe, Aghadoe,
On Shaun Dhu,* my mother's son in Aghadoe!
When your throat fries in hell's drouth, salt the flame be in
    your mouth,
For the treachery you did in Aghadoe.

For they tracked me to that glen in Aghadoe, Aghadoe,
When the price was on his head in Aghadoe:
O'er the mountain, through the wood, as I stole to him with
    food,
Where in hiding lone he lay in Aghadoe.

But they never took him living in Aghadoe, Aghadoe;
With the bullets in his heart in Aghadoe,
There he lay, the head, my breast keeps the warmth of where
    'twould rest,
Gone, to win the traitor's gold, from Aghadoe!

I walked to Mallow town from Aghadoe, Aghadoe,
Brought his head from the jail's gate to Aghadoe;
Then I covered him with fern, and I piled on him the cairn,
Like an Irish King he sleeps in Aghadoe.

* Shaun Dhu: Black-haired John

O, to creep into that cairn in Aghadoe, Aghadoe!
There to rest upon his breast in Aghadoe!
Sure your dog for you could die with no truer heart that I,
Your own love, cold on your cairn in Aghadoe.

JOHN TODHUNTER

Indexes

Indexes

Author Index

Title Index